About the Author

B. D. Gibson has worn many hats in his career before returning to writing. After taking a small writing course he decided to write from within, rather than use a formula. He is a classically trained oil painter as well as a chartered herbalist. He enjoys writing and hopes to produce more works.

Dedication

This book is dedicated to my sister, Rita Jordan (Nee Gibson) for always believing in me.

Bryan Dennis Gibson

CRY OF FREEDOM

AUSTIN MACAULEY
PUBLISHERS LTD.

A CIP catalogue record for this title is available from the British Library.

ISBN 978 1 78554 295 4 (paperback)
ISBN 978 1 78554 296 1 (hardback)
ISBN 978 1 78554 297 8 (E-Book)

www.austinmacauley.com

First Published (2016)
Austin Macauley Publishers Ltd.
25 Canada Square
Canary Wharf
London
E14 5LB

Acknowledgments

I would like to acknowledge Robert MacFarlane for his help with getting this book launched. I would also like to thank the staff of Austin Macauley for their generous help and support. Special thanks to Tom Haynes to had to put up with my limited computer skills.

CONTENTS

CRY OF FREEDOM

John Cameron smelled the smoke of oily torches burning long before he heard the clash of swords or the screams of dying men. Dressing, he quickly reached for his sword and ran towards the source of the commotion. It was nearly midnight and parts of his castle that were now on fire began to light up the night sky casting ominous shadows on the castle walls. The only question on John's mind was, who was attacking, and why? He was at peace with his fellow clansmen and neighbours. This made no sense!

Quickly he saw that it was a Norse attack, and this group was a mix of Norse-Irish, Scottish outlaws, with a mix of assorted fugitives and trash from across the islands. They followed a new leader and a new banner. A large chain-mailed warrior appeared out of the shadows barring John's way and nearly impaling him with his spear in the process. He had a difficult fight with this one and after being cut several times managed to dispatch his foe.

One of John's archers took out an axe-wielding warrior that was charging at him. It was a difficult shot in the half-light and John would reward this archer later, he thought to himself as he searched for his next opponent. Grabbing a fallen Norseman's shield he charged around a corner surprising two advancing men who hesitated for a moment thinking he was one of them. That moment's hesitation cost them their lives as John sent them to meet Odin.

The plot was now revealed and this made his blood boil. He was not prepared for an attack by his own brother. They had never been the best of friends and John knew that William had always been jealous of his throne but to do this was utter madness. John was soon thrust into the group surrounding William. He slashed, thrust, twisted, and turned but was eventually cut down. John did manage to slay two of his attackers and wound a third before he was cut down.

As he lay dying thinking of his wife and children, William rode over to his brother, leaned over and said, "You should have seen this coming, my brother. You are not worthy to be king. Your throne and your wife are rightly mine. I will enjoy them both."

With his last dying breath John cursed him, "Go to hell. I will be avenged, my son will kill you one day."

William could only laugh. He had other plans for John's son and his daughters.

Sixteen year old James Cameron would remember this night and the last conversation he had with his father.

"Death comes to us all," spoke John Cameron. "We Celts do not fear it as other men do for we know that life is but a circle and all men return in another form, another life, another form, another time."

James would remember and think of those words in the days to come while he was chained to his oar contemplating death.

Shortly after this encounter John came upon a group of men being led by his own brother. He watched in disbelief as William put to the sword a clansman that had saved his life in battle, and now served in John's guard. The plot now revealed John's blood began to boil. They had never been close brothers and John was aware that William had always been jealous of his throne, but to do this was utter madness.

A furious John attacked the group and slashed, thrusted, and twisted and turned, cutting down four of them before he was overcome. It was a valiant effort. As he lay dying his thought were of his wife and children, when William rode over to him and said, "You should have seen this coming, my brother. You are not worthy to be a king, you are weak. Your throne and your wife are rightly mine and I will enjoy them both."

With his last dying breath John cursed his. "Go to hell… I will be avenged, my son will kill you one day."

William could only laugh for he had other plans for John's sons and daughters. Fourteen year old James Cameron would remember this night and the last serious conversation he had with his father.

"Death comes to us all," spoke John Cameron. "We Celts do not fear it as other men do for we know that life is but a circle and all men return, in another form, in another life, and in another time."

James would remember and think of those words in the days to come while chained to his oar contemplating death.

While enduring the lash and the constant beat that pounded out the stroke and speed of the living hell he would endure for the next three years, a king would be forged.

For two days they marched south. It was slow going as the ground was very rocky and hilly; it gradually levelled out as they neared a small rarely used anchorage eastern shore of a small bay.

This was unfamiliar territory to James. He had never been that far south; at sixteen he was not yet a travelled man.

Most of this territory 'James' or 'Jamie' as he liked to be called was similar to home and he was impressed by the size of the yew and oak trees he saw along the way. He had never such large ones.

Marched to this place and chained together like animals he, his cousins Liam and Wolf, a cousin by his father's sister and many young girls and playmates awaited their fate. They had no idea of where they were going or what fate had in store for them. Sometimes it is better not to know. The one thing they did know for sure was that they were scared.

An encampment was made, guards were put out and fires were built, soon the slaves would be fed. Tired, dirty, hungry and near exhaustion this ragged band of captives were fed a thin soup and a small chunk of bread, both greedily devoured.

Their new masters would keep them tired and hungry for tired and hungry slaves were less trouble, more obedient, and less apt to try and escape.

Before the soft glow of the morning sunrise broke over the horizon Jamie managed to get close enough to his cousin Liam to ask if he knew what had happened. They had been separated during the march and this was the first time they were able to talk. Jamie had no recollection of what happened as he was clubbed over the head shortly after rising; the attack woke him up.

Liam couldn't tell him very much as he had been clubbed over the head as well. Most of what he gathered came from his fellow captives, and from his brother Fergus. Speaking softly so the guards wouldn't hear them, he informed Jamie that his father was dead but he knew nothing of the fate of his mother and sister.

It was a plot instigated by their Uncle William of that much he was sure. The previous night before the attack Liam had been awakened by a loud argument coming from his uncle's chamber. Seeing the light coming from his uncle's chamber he crept close to hear better but couldn't get too close for fear of being discovered. What he heard didn't make much sense either.

Liam couldn't make out a lot of what they were saying but his uncle was arguing with two large Norsemen wearing skins.

From what he could hear he gathered that several small gold mines had been discovered, but he couldn't hear where they were, and assumed that the mines were close or on their father's land. To Liam this seemed impossible; that these mines were discovered at the same time, on two different islands.

The conversation soon died out and the warriors made a toast and then departed in haste.

Liam assumed the warriors left with messages for William's friends and he didn't know what to do. He was scared and confused over what he had heard and went back to bed not sure if he was dreaming or awake. He further stated that some of the captives told him that many had been put to the sword, and many were slain in a savage manner and this was all he could tell Jamie.

Shortly before the camp roused they agreed to try and stick together and look after each other. Their only concern for the moment was that Wolf hadn't shown up yet and this worried them. After camp had broken they were marched south for several hours and after many miles they stopped at a small sheltered cove where they waited under the hot midday sun.

More prisoners were brought in and Liam and Jamie were in better spirits when they discovered that Wolf was among the prisoners. They were now together along with Liam's brother Fergus and some friends. The thing most on Liam's mind was that Fergus had never been in good health and was always a sickly child, who was now a long way from home and care. Seeing Fergus and Wolf did make him feel better and he became less afraid.

After four or five hours of waiting a large vessel followed by various sleek vessels appeared on the horizon. They had never seen ships like this before and soon they were close enough to drop anchor, and various small launches headed toward the beach. Greetings were exchanged and after much talk fires were lit and food prepared. A copious amount of wine was consumed by the pirates as the trio of princes awaited their new life as galley slaves.

These pirates were a rough, tough hard fighting group that lived and fought hard because they knew the sea was a cruel mistress and their time on earth would be short at best. They dressed in all manner of costumes; some wore turbans of silk adorned with feathers and jewels. Many wore large gold and silver earrings and many were tattooed and battle scarred. All were men of the sea.

The next morning the prisoners were shuttled over to the larger vessels. This ship boasted over a hundred rowers and could outrun many of the ships at sea. The smaller vessels were very fast and they would eventually be transferred to one of these once they reached their destination. Jamie was impressed by the sails that were emblazoned with large birds of prey on them.

This ship they would call home for the next three years sailed alongside them as they headed for an unknown destination in distant lands. It would be here during their formative years that they would learn to endure the cruelty of men. They learned to bare the sting of the lash and whip and to endure a multitude of other indignities that would be heaped upon them during the coming years.

Kingships would be driven into these young princes over time, and they would learn to endure physical as well as mental pain. They would learn the twin lessons of patience and perseverance, and of what the real meaning of injustice was. The most important lesson they would earn is that all men whether slave or king had worth and importance and should be judged accordingly.

The cruelty of the pirates and guards showed the worst side of men, for lust, greed and brutality ruled their lives. Fights often broke out among the slaves as well as the pirates, and they were nearly always to the death. The lessons these three young men were learning cannot be taught in the courts of the nobles, they must be experienced in the arena of life.

"I do not like what I see in the hearts of men," Jamie mused while rowing one day. "Could these things be replaced by courage, loyalty, honour and justice, or are all men beyond redemption?" He would not find the answer to this question for many years. One thing he had made up his mind on was that if and when he had reclaimed his throne he would rule in a just and fair manner just as his father had done.

Jamie also made a private vow to himself that any man that broke this sacred trust would feel the edge of his sword across his throat. How or when Jamie would accomplish this he didn't know, but it was a belief that he held true and it would help sustain him during the coming years.

While each of these young men settled into the life they were now chained to, they still dreamed of running, playing and fishing in the hills and valleys and streams of their home. Alas each knew that this dream was gone forever, but not from their hearts. Each of them also decided that those responsible for this forced exile would pay with their lives.

Each of them prayed to the gods for this chance, and strangely one of them must have been listening this day.

While the prisoners were being rowed back to the large ship the last sound Jamie would remember was the piercing sound of the black ravens that were scavenging the abandoned pirate encampment on the beach. The sound haunted him and he decided that if he returned this would be his battle cry and war emblem. His enemies would come to fear this cry.

The men who stole his birthright would come to regret this day he promised, this would be his personal cry of freedom. On the second night of their voyage they would learn the terrible price that freedom costs, but for now they would try and sleep. Sleep came easy to them, for they were worn out from their arduous journey and beatings endured.

It was a different story at Liam's father's castle, Cormac O'Connor was a better general than William, and after his spies had reported that they had heard of some shifting clan loyalty and of following a different banner than his own, he doubled the guard, sent for more reinforcements of men he could trust.

What Cormac didn't know was that Sean O'Reagan had made different plans, and many of Cormac's allies had already been bought or killed by William. There were some of Cormac's allies that would remain loyal and some that William couldn't attack until he had built up his army. This bothered him because even when his plans were complete his hold on the new territories he was controlling would be tenuous at best. He needed time.

O'Reagan and Cormac had been friends many years ago, but parted company over some mischance and had not spoken for many years. William and Sean decided that an attack straight on the castle wouldn't work. The only way to overtake it was by subterfuge and stealth. Many of those that rode with O'Reagan were William's Norse friends and upon seeing the Norse the alarm would be raised and the element of surprise would be lost.

Cormac's castle was a medium sized castle and it was well guarded by seasoned warriors. This would not be an easy fight. It had been decided that O'Reagan and a small retinue of men would beg food and shelter for the night. While the attention of the guards was focused on the new arrivals the Norse would silently scale the castle walls and wait for Sean's signal to attack.

Cormac greeted his old friend with some suspicion, it had been many years since they had talked, and he wondered what the urgency was now.

"What brings you to my castle at this hour, Sean?" he asked.

"Is that any way for two old friends to greet one another?" Sean replied. "I've been travelling and arrived late at my destination, we seek only shelter for the night." Saying this he stepped forward as if to greet Cormac and with one deft move brought his sword up and drove it through Cormac's chest. He fell to the floor with a stunned look on his face and then collapsed.

The noise was like a signal to the Norse on the walls and they attacked only to be met by the unexpected fury of Cormac's men. They were expecting an easy victory and weren't counting on fierce resistance. O'Reagan and his allies were beginning to lose ground, they were in trouble. Many of O'Reagan's men had been forced outside the castle doors and joined those already fighting in the courtyard.

The day would have been in Cormac's favour had a large troop of Norse not ridden in. The tide of battle turned in O'Reagan's favour but it was a hard fought battle that lasted for nearly three hours. The battle for this castle cost many lives and many of his men were bruised and battered. This was a setback.

Sean would have to petition William for more men, he needed time to rebuild his forces and until then was at William's bidding. For now he needed his support.

Sean was no fool, right now William was holding all the cards and he would have to play along for the moment. He held no delusions about their alliance or of William's loyalty. Gold was gold, but that didn't mean he had to trust him, and he didn't. He only hoped that William would one day have an attack of madness and challenge him to a sword fight. He would see to it that it was a short fight, he thought to himself.

Sean gathered a large share of the mine since it bordered his land and William and his troops saw to its operation and distribution. Sean's men would report to him any discrepancy. The count was always accurate as far as he knew.

This was an easy time for William to achieve his goals for most of the kingdoms in the British Isles were merely a collection of petty kingdoms. There had been no great unification as yet and borders and alliances shifted around like the winds.

O'Reagan had never liked the fact that William relied on his Norse friends for support. No one trusted them and they were growing stronger and more organised as the years went on. These wild warriors were getting bolder and plundering at will in ever wider reaches.

DANEMARK

William's interest in Wolf's father's kingdom was not very great for his only interest would be the outlying ports and mines that supplied steel for his weapons makers, and a few small coal mines.

Most of the areas that William had interest or influence in were on the outlying edges of Olaf's kingdom and were easily overtaken, and lightly defended. Wolf's abduction and kidnapping had been unexpected, as William didn't know he was staying at the Camerons, and to keep Olaf off guard sent a force to attack his village. It offered no military value.

The Norse attacked Olaf's village a few weeks after things had settled down in Scotland. It was a cool fall day and the alarm was given before the Norse could surprise Olaf and his men. The Norse were attacking battle hardened warriors like themselves and they had no fear of William's allies. Olaf still raided and traded in a wide area and his men's reflexes were razor sharp. William lost this one.

Olaf for his part couldn't understand why the Norse would attack him. His reputation as a warrior was known far and wide and most of the Norse gave him a wide berth. Olaf knew nothing of the uprisings in Scotland and Ireland and any news would take a long time to reach him. His outlying mines and ports he rarely visited any more so their loss would be insignificant.

Olaf's main mines and ports were still under his control and would remain that way. William was smart enough to know that he couldn't pressure Olaf too much as the man could raise a large army if required and he couldn't engage in open warfare yet. He needed a steady supply of weapons and he needed time to build his army. For the moment he would tread lightly.

Olaf would never believe William's story that the Norse had attacked his brother's castle and taken the boys as captives. If Olaf ever learned that William was responsible for his son's disappearance he would rouse half his nation and kill William with his own hands, but he could never prove it.

His kingdom was intact for the moment, there had been some damage to it but this was easily restored and it would be some time before he learned of Wolf's fate. The news would not please him but for now he only hoped that Wolf and his cousins were safe. He knew John Cameron would defend and look after Wolf as he did his own son.

In later years it always bothered him that John would pay with his life defending his home and castle. The stories that were being told around campfires throughout the land over John's final battle at the castle, and the fight at Cormac's castle did make him very proud. They were told wherever he travelled and he never got tired of hearing them.

THE TERROR

The terrors began when the young girls that had reached puberty were taken first. They were subjected to indignities, which few could imagine. Quite a number of them died during the night, and the rest were bleeding and suffering from shock.

These three future kings were forced to listen to the cries and screams of their friends, neighbours and family members.

They could do nothing to help as they were chained to their oars and forced to row to a steady beat or lashed if they didn't. Death came to many of these innocent victims and to know they were helpless to do anything about it bothered them and would haunt their dreams for many years to come.

The Barbary Coast pirates were among the most savage and cruel pirates on the seas. The Barbary Coast contained many small streams and natural harbours, which they made the most use of, creating bases and safe havens for their vessels.

Very few of the ruling powers had large navies or armies so the pirates did pretty much as they pleased and raided wherever they wanted with little worry of capture. They had to be a hard crew of sailors in order to survive the harsh life and savage seas. For sport the pirates threw the bodies of the dead overboard and then bet on which shark would take which body. This was a ghastly sight to witness.

This was a baneful crew and on the second night of the voyage they introduced a new form of terror to their helpless victims. The victims wondered if God had abandoned them and why?

On the second night of the voyage, while in a drunken rage the pirates turned on the pre-pubescent boys. They were taken repeatedly and the victims' screams could be heard piercing the blackness of the night for what seemed like hours, unknown to Liam his younger brother Fergus was one of those screaming.

Fergus was only eleven years old and small of stature. He was taken repeatedly by the overseer Jaffar and his cronies. Left in a heap on the floor he discovered a knife dropped by one of his attackers. When he felt able to move again he charged out of the galley and seeing Jaffar at the rear of the vessel came at him screaming and cursing.

Hearing the commotion behind him Jaffar suddenly turned around sword drawn and found Fergus impaled on it. No one was more surprised that Jaffar; it had all happened so suddenly. Fergus fell back onto the deck and with his last dying words turned to Liam and said, "Don't tell anybody what they did to me." He then gasped and fell to the deck, and was gone.

The three cousins stared at each other in disbelief. They were in shock over what they had witnessed, everything had happened so fast. No one moved for a while and then Fergus and any other bodies were thrown overboard. Liam noticed the blood which stained the back of his brother's breeches and now he understood what the pirates did to him. These are not men, Liam thought to himself, they are savage beasts. His anger boiling, he vowed to revenge his brother for this night. His smouldering eyes then turned to Jaffar.

Liam's eyes locked on to Jaffar's, they radiated an intense glow that seemed to burn from somewhere deep inside him. This mesmerising quality would in future unnerve many of the men he faced in battle. This quality would become part of his legend.

Jamie was as outraged as Liam over what had happened and they both had struggled in vain with their chains to try and help. He liked Fergus and he didn't deserve to die like that.

Now Jamie had a big problem. If Liam ever got the chance to get Jaffar alone he would kill him for sure, with his bare hands if necessary or convenient. This he couldn't allow, not until they had some sort of plan worked out.

It was a hopeless situation, chained to an oar there was little they could do about it for now. Jamie's hatred for his uncle was at fever pitch and he made a personal vow to himself that William Cameron would pay for his treachery. This burning hatred in these three would help keep them alive in the coming years of pain and peril.

The one saving grace on board ship was the rowers were well fed and rested. The pirates were smart enough to know that weak tired, sickly rowers couldn't propel a ship very far or fast.

The pirates needed both speed and power in critical situations they got both, with strong healthy rowers. This did not spare anyone from the lash or other forms of abuse. Often healthy rowers would be sold off when the pirates had more slaves than gold. Many of their friends had suffered this fate.

For nearly three years they went all through the Mediterranean, down the coast of Africa and beyond, raiding and looting at will. Twice the vessels they were chained to were lost in skirmishes at sea. Each time they survived, and with each new day's rowing new muscles were being used and strengthened, and stretched to the limit. Along with these new forms of pain and anguish they learned to bear the lash and beatings that were handed out on a regular basis. They were growing tougher.

The trio were amongst the strongest if not the strongest rowers aboard ship. Most of the overseers left them alone now for the harsh life they were thrust into had transformed them from boys into large aggressive men. The greatest change took place in Wolf for now he was nearly six feet, eight inches tall and weighed in at around two hundred and eighty-five pounds of rock solid muscle. The other two had the bodies of Greek athletes and were not over six feet tall themselves and ready for a fight.

Time had brought many changes to these young boys who had grown into men. While chained to their oars they taught each other four different languages: Gaelic, English, Danish and Farsi.

Each could also understand bits and pieces of other dialects and languages. Liam knew how to write in the script of the church and had been given some medical knowledge by his mother; she had been shown by her uncle Donal the Druid priest. They taught themselves verbally by writing and drawing in the filth of the galley floor.

Finally they decided it was time for what they knew would be a risky adventure. A plan they knew had little chance of success but one they had to take. They had grown tired of being slaves and decided to try and escape. Where they would escape to they didn't know. At this point in time they didn't care either.

The sultan's fleet did little to discourage piracy on the seas, and the pirates themselves preferred to attack rich merchant vessels anyway. The rewards were greater and the pickings were easier than attacking the sultan's fleet. His ships usually contained armed troops that had no love for the pirates, and if the pirates' attack failed the penalty would be too severe. Each gave the other a wide berth.

The pirates unloaded plunder and took on supplies whenever they landed in a neutral port. This day more than the usual amount of supplies had been loaded and the trio thought they had a long voyage ahead to South Africa perhaps. While in port the pirates rendezvoused with two other larger ships and then sailed off into the night.

The excitement and chatter amongst the pirates and crew was heard by the captives who understood that they were to attack and plunder a large ship carrying an ample treasure, as well as a member of the Persian royal family to hold for ransom.

The men that had paid for this expected results, the rest was all a bonus for them. The vessel was to be destroyed and sunk after the pirates were done with it and the treasure unloaded onto the two larger ships they rendezvoused with earlier.

The human cargo was to be put on this ship and then the three were to split up and meet at an assigned port only the captains knew of. That night the ship that held Jamie and his cousins would vanish forever, as would any ship on the waters that night.

Shortly after dawn the next day two vessels were sighted coming from the east and as they drew nearer it was confirmed the ships were flying the flag of Persia. The sultan's ships were no doubt armed with soldiers but since none of his ships were ever attacked by the pirates they wouldn't be expecting this. The pirates' eyes were glowing with delight as they dreamed of all the gold and plunder they would take home this day.

The pirates would fly a flag they captured from Aza's new husband's fleet and those on board the princess' vessel would think it was the prince sending a welcoming commission to greet them. The attack would begin as soon as the sultan's ships drew nearer... but something else was drawing near, a storm of savage proportions.

The calm winds and soft golden glow of the morning soon changed to a darkened, black, foreboding sky. The winds began to blow hard from the north and thunder could be heard rolling in, mixed with flashes of lightning and rain. The sea began to churn and boil, soon the waves began to crest, and the pirate craft began to bounce along the waves with a nauseating rhythm. The waves were beginning to increase in size and power, and there was little they could do to keep the ship out of harm's way. They unchained the slaves, for every man was needed to try and keep the vessel afloat.

Trying to keep afloat in this kind of storm was futile; if a man went overboard he was swallowed up by the sea and there would be no rescue. The main mast snapped first. The crew had only taken the sail halfway down when a savage blast of wind hit them tossing men into the sea and killing others when it hit the deck.

The second and third smaller masts went next, and when the steering snapped, they were completely helpless now.

It was only a matter of time before the vessel was hit by a huge wave. Amazingly it survived, but another blow like that would shatter it into pieces.

They were being tossed about like corks in a barrel. Jamie grabbed Wolf and Liam and suggested they grab something to float with and some sort of gear to survive with. Wolf grabbed a knife, Liam managed to grab a couple of water skins, and Jamie snatched a bag of biscuits. They jumped together and tried to stay close when they hit the water.

With horror they watched as a huge wave smashed the ship to bits. They couldn't see anything of the sultan's ships and presumed they suffered the same fate as they.

For many years to come, people would talk of this night of storms and death. The whole Mediterranean region and coastal settlements were ravaged and many lives lost to the storm.

The three princes clinging to the wreckage could only pray that they would survive the night.

Storms were a part of life at sea but even seasoned men of the sea were always astonished at how a clear blue sky with a gentle breeze could change into a savage nightmare that forced a man to fight all night to stay afloat and alive. Even if the crew could find shelter in a cove or bay the ship was still tossed around by the sea causing much damage. Often they would have to wait in some barren cove while repairs were done to the vessel.

During one violent storm off the coast of North Africa the boat capsized and the whole crew had their first bath in a long time. This sort of thing went on all the time and every time it did the trio was scared out of their wits. As slaves they faced other risks for if it were a choice between losing their lives or losing some slaves chained to their oars, the choice was obvious, they were only slaves after all.

The pirates were able to commandeer a ship or arrange passage to where they could get to where their new ships were being built usually in fairly short order, and it was business as usual. The pirates were cruel and ruthless but they weren't stupid. Twice they attacked vessels that were carrying large quantities of gold and silver coins, as well as slaves.

The pirate's treasure was often used to buy bigger and faster ships for the pirate fleet, and some of the loot was used to buy taverns and coastal property. This would give some legitimacy to their enterprises and give them bases to operate from at the same time.

This night of terror was not the only one they would have to endure during their forced confinement and slavery. There would be many times during the following years when there was little food or water. Often the pirates ventured into new territory and never seemed to have enough supplies to finish the journey. On several voyages the pirates that controlled this area decided to attack, and once or twice were nearly overtaken.

Sometimes it would be the sailors of the nearest ruling potentate's navy that would attack and at other times it would be groups or individual pirate vessels that attacked them. The renegade pirates were the worst and often attacked in groups. The pirates often fought duels to the death with each other so it was no surprise that they would turn on each other while at sea.

During one particularly nasty skirmish off the West Coast of Africa a mast broke off during and fell crashing through the deck and collapsed a beam directly overhead of Jamie and Liam. This dragged them both under the water that was now rushing in. Wolf and Eskandar, a giant of a black man they had befriended managed to lift the beam off allowing them to get free. On three occasions a pirate vessel equipped with a ramming prow smashed through the side of their ship nearly killing Wolf and Eskandar.

The most consistent danger they faced was the sea itself for the weather and moods of the sea could change in an instant. When the seas raged and boiled the slaves were released from the chains holding them for every man was needed to keep the vessel afloat.

Disease would often take some of the crew members without warning and then spread to the others. This was a very great fear for these three young princes for this they could not fight. The pirates could hold their own applying battlefield medicine and a few were fair surgeons in their own right. Their experience came from repetition rather than from knowledge.

Once this trio was in danger of breaking up after the pirate captain decided to gamble Wolf to a rival captain while playing a game of chance. Although strong galley slaves were important to the ship they were still considered property and the trio had seen other slaves sold off or traded. Fortunately lady luck was with their captain and he won the game. Had he lost they might never have seen Wolf again. This was something they couldn't allow.

After this episode Jamie and his cousins decided that it was time to escape as they reasoned the odds were running against them anyway. Sooner or later something would happen that they would end up split apart and Jamie wasn't going to let this happen. Their only chance of surviving this and returning to put to the sword to the people that caused their enslavement was to stick together.

The first thing they had to decide was the age-old questions; when and how? And where would they escape to? They couldn't break away by sea unless they could steal a small boat, but this would have lessened their chances for making a successful escape. Their only chance was when the pirates docked or took on water or traded goods. Their best chance would be when the pirates returned to their strongholds, it was a small chance at best.

The first thing they needed to make their escape was a key, for if they couldn't get out of their chains, they really couldn't get very far. The guards kept a close eye on their keys as they would have to try and fashion one. Scrounging the bits of steel needed to make one wouldn't be difficult, but trying to fashion and fit a key would be a difficult task. They would only be able to work on it while the pirates were docked and drunk, and even then it would be risky.

Many months of painstaking scraping and filing finally produced a set of keys that worked, each rower was chained with an individual lock, and then all were chained together in series to an individual post. They would have to work on numerous locks at the same time. It seemed like an impossible task.

They had to hide their keys and hope none were discovered before their escape. In a few more weeks they would be docking at one of the pirate captain's strongholds, and that would be when they would attempt their escape, and break for freedom. Jamie was worried that if their escape failed the pirates would kill them outright.

It was decided this way because they had too many close calls and figured it was only a matter of time before something split them apart and this they couldn't allow, their uncle had to be paid back for his treachery. There would be no room for error, and they were getting frustrated, impatient, and worrisome, not knowing what the fates had in store for them.

The exact time of their incarceration was eleven hundred and fifty-three days. As it came closer to the night of escape the three young princes made a pact between themselves. They agreed that if their escape was successful they would never again take their freedom for granted and whenever possible they would free very slave that they could, by whatever means necessary.

As he gazed up at the darkening sky and watched as the stars vanished behind the clouds, Jamie wondered if they would ever return home or would they survive at all. Jamie's questions would soon be answered by Mother Nature, only it was not the answer he was expecting. Within a few short hours they would be fighting for their lives again, with no real chance of winning, only luck would decide their fate.

THE RAFT

As the black of night gave way to the morning light; the sea began to calm down for a short while. The young princes were able to see the extent of the storms fury. Debris, broken masts, and torn sails were scattered everywhere, amidst the floating and broken bodies of the pirate ship's crew. The damage was of the extent that it looked as if the ship had been picked up and smacked on the water over and over again, much like a young child that gets mad at a toy and smashes it to pieces.

When the trio went overboard they managed to swim to a large piece of broken mast and cling on. They had to survive together. They saw two other bodies hanging onto another broken mast and were able to swim over to them. To their surprise it was Jamshid, and Eskandar. Jamshid was a thief who stole from the wrong person and ended up as a galley slave. On board he was always stealing small little things from the guards and generally causing trouble.

Eskandar was a giant of a black man who was a king in his own country before being captured and sold into slavery. It was Eskandar that fascinated the trio the most for he was midnight black from head to foot, was bald, and had piercing reddish eyes that could almost look into a man's soul. They had never seen a black man before and had no idea that such people existed.

His colour didn't matter to them; they were friends and for the moment they were free. They were all happy that they survived for now the odds of survival were better.

Every member of this ragged crew had sailed these seas many times before but in the darkness and confusion they had no way of getting their bearings. They had no idea of where they were or where they would go if they did escape.

Each member drank some water from the barrel, it had a slightly salty taste to it; but it was quite drinkable. Sitting there discussing their situation several ideas were proposed and adopted such as using short lengths of rope to fasten themselves to the raft in case anyone was washed overboard. All agreed.

This was a decision that would prove invaluable during the next few hours as the violent seas began to churn again and the rains and storm returned with a renewed fury. The little raft bounced and bobbed around with each rising swell. They had done a good job on the raft for it held together and kept them out of the water.

Several hours later when the seas calmed, the rains had left, the winds died away as fast as they came. A tired crew could now get some rest and they were soon fast asleep, staying that way for many hours. When they awoke it was to a calm sea and an overcast sky. They could relax for a while.

They discovered that water from the rainstorm had gathered in some of the pockets of the canvas and this was quickly added to the barrel. Their main concern now was for food as they hadn't eaten for two days, and the growling of stomachs on board was growing. The food they had tried to bring with them was lost at sea. They would have to forage to survive.

"Now that we are all together," Jamie spoke up and said, "we need to somehow grasp as many of these broken masts, timbers, and anything else that will float and lash some sort of raft together for we can't stay in this cold water much longer."

"Aye," Liam responded. "We can't survive this for very long, my legs are already starting to get numb."

It was decided that since Jamie, Eskandar and Wolf were the strongest swimmers they would do the gathering, and Jamshid and Liam would assemble and lash it together. After an hour or so of herculean effort a large raft about fifteen by twenty was fashioned that sat about two feet above sea level. Three very tired swimmers pulled themselves on board.

For the next two hours this tired and ragged crew of slaves strengthened and secured the raft for they feared the storm would rear up again. Their fears were justified. This was an area known for the fierce gales that swept over the seas but this one was an unprecedented occurrence.

Catching some of the floating debris as it went by they were able to scrounge a small barrel half full of water, and were able to fashion a steering rudder for the raft. Jamie and Eskandar rigged up a shelter out of sailcloth, and fashioned a small sail to use when the weather calmed down. The shelter would provide some respite from the elements. Would it be enough?

Once they had finished these chores this exhausted group of survivors collapsed and slept for the next six hours waking to dark and ominous looking skies.

Sometime later Wolf called to the others as he noticed a pile of floating debris with some bodies coming near them and Wolf volunteered to investigate. He was a strong swimmer but even so attached a long rope around his waist and swam towards the floating pile.

Once Wolf had reached the mass of wreckage he found three people, one dead, one unconscious, and one alive but bleeding badly. Wolf knew from many voyages with his father that it would be only a matter of time before the sharks smelled the blood from the woman's wound on her leg.

Leaving the dead woman he fastened the rope to the floating mass and signalled for them to pull him in quickly. Wolf had barely reached the raft with his human cargo when the first large dorsal fins began to appear. The sharks quickly devoured the dead servant and nervously circled the raft.

Once on board Liam attended the woman's wound and bound them with strips of linen torn from her dress. Having some knowledge of medicine he was concerned about her loss of blood and her pulse was very weak. The cold water had probably slowed the loss of blood somewhat and she was young. For now they could only wait.

The other woman was beginning to regain consciousness but was unable to speak and soon slipped back into sleep again.

This was a turn of events they hadn't expected.

Eskandar was the first to comment to Wolf. "Remind me the next time I go fishing to take you along with me, for in all my years of fishing, I have never been able to pull two beautiful women out of the sea, all I ever got was fish."

They all laughed uncontrollably for the next few minutes.

Once they had gained control of themselves again they decided to try and catch some fish as hunger was gnawing at them all, and the food that Liam had grabbed when they went overboard was lost in the storm. Immediately they went to work fashioning some line using the ropes they had secured from the ship, for hooks they used some bent nails and the princess's earring were used for a lure.

Within twenty-five minutes Wolf and Eskandar managed to land around fifteen medium and small fish. Wolf figured that the raft must have floated over a passing school of fish otherwise they wouldn't have caught so many, it was pure luck.

The starving group of survivors soon had the fish cleaned and them Jamie spoke up. "I've never eaten raw fish before and we have nothing to cook with, what do we do now?"

The group then decided to squeeze as much oil out of the fish as they could and try to drink it, but this didn't work out too well as they all gagged on the first swallow. It was then decided to slice the fish as thinly as possible and hang the strips in the sun to dry out figuring this would make a more palatable meal. In a few hours they would eat for the first time in days.

The fish dried out and after consuming most of the fish that had been caught, sleep came upon them. They kept a small portion of fish aside for when the women were able to eat. The unconscious woman revived but was too weak to eat so Liam gave her some water and told her to suck on the piece of dried fish for its juices would nourish her.

Liam couldn't help but notice that she and the princess were both very beautiful women. Once she had regained some strength she told them in Farsi that the bleeding woman was Princess Aza, the only daughter of the Sultan of Persia. They were on their way to the prince's kingdom to meet and arrange their upcoming wedding ceremonies.

She told Liam her name was Sarah and that she had only been Aza's servant for a couple of years and she worried that if they weren't rescued it would mean war between the two countries.

The princess's new husband was a rich and powerful warrior king and would be worried about the fate of his new bride. This marriage was supposed to ease the tensions between the two kingdoms and restore order.

Liam then told Sarah about the attempted kidnap plot of the pirates and what they were paid by someone in the sultan's court. She knew nothing of this but was not surprised as the sultan's court was filled with traitors and evil men. Sarah had an idea of who they were but dared not say anything in fear of her life.

The storm had blown them off course but the ship's captain had weathered it well and was starting to make some headway before a succession of large waves finally sank the vessel.

The princess awoke a few hours later and drank some water and sucked on a little dried fish. She was still very weak, in fact both of the women were. Sarah appeared to be suffering from a mild concussion but had no external injuries.

Princess Aza learned of the story of their rescue from Sarah and of these wild young galley slaves who had saved their lives. Since she was now awake and feeling a little better

Liam crawled over to her to check on her arm and leg and was quickly slapped and admonished for touching her.

"Do not touch me infidel, I am the Princess Aza, daughter of the Sultan of Persia and no one but the royal court physician may touch me, especially where you are now touching me."

Liam responded by giving the princess a small backhand across the face. Aza froze and glared at Liam as her face turned red.

"You may be a princess in your land but in case you haven't noticed we aren't anywhere near your land," Liam told her. "I am going to tend and redress your wounds whether you like it or not. As for your court physician you can send for him any time you like."

Even the princess started to give a feeble laugh at this, and she was soon asleep. Liam was worried the wound might be infected and he was glad the princess had passed out so he could inspect and treat the wound properly.

When the princess awoke later, Jamie questioned her learning more of her voyage and of her future husband. He learned that she had not seen him for about ten years and that she had loved him as a childhood friend but wasn't sure how she would feel now. Ten years was a long time; people changed.

Before she passed out again she found herself being drawn towards this savage from another land who spoke her own language as well as she did. He was beginning to stir up strange emotions within her and she was becoming confused over it all. After questioning Aza, Jamie pondered the fate of this makeshift crew and of how he could somehow turn this situation to their advantage.

Jamie watched the princess sleeping for a while and he couldn't help but notice how beautiful and curvaceous she was.

To the best of his knowledge she was probably the best looking woman he had ever seen. He wasn't aware of it at the moment but the seeds of romance were firmly planted in him. Aza was of medium height, around five feet ten with long black hair and a slender build. The colour of her skin was the colour of almonds and she had piercing black eyes.

To say that she was beginning to stir emotions in him would be an understatement, he was already in love with her he just didn't know it yet.

By the fourth day of their raft voyage the water was getting low and what little food they had left was nearly gone. Some had been set-aside for the women who were in a much more weakened condition.

The raft passengers were getting tired of eating dried fish and surviving on a few sips of water per day. They were a group nearly at the end of their ropes. They had reasoned that because of the storm's fury they might never be rescued, as many ships even those securely tied up in safe harbours were likely to be damaged. In fact there were few ships in seaworthy condition anywhere on the seas, hope was dwindling.

The sun beat down on them by day and the chill of night forced them to try and stay covered most of the time in order to survive the elements. They were weakening. On the sixth day of their ordeal Eskandar spotted a small dot on the horizon as the sun climbed to noon and it was moving slowly towards them.

The vessel was coming closer and any of the crew that had the strength tried to signal them by waving pieces of sailcloth or strips of bright cloth torn from the women's dresses.

They were spotted and when the ship got close the sails were dropped and a small rowboat manned by four oarsmen came alongside. Seeing the condition of the survivors they were quickly but carefully loaded into the rowboat and brought back to the main vessel.

At last they were rescued and each person thanked the gods they prayed to. It was a miracle that any of them survived.

Wolf threw the princess over his shoulder, and Eskandar did the same with Sarah and with difficulty they climbed aboard. As soon as everyone was on board the captain ordered the sails unfurled and they changed course.

The captain had one more port to visit, to pick up supplies and fresh water before returning to Persia. It was only by chance they were in the area. The captain and crew were returning from a trading mission for the sultan and the ships holds were full of gold, spices, rare wood and all manner of merchandise.

This was the largest merchant vessel the trio had ever seen. In fact it was the largest ship sailing these waters and displaced several tons of cargo. She had been hidden in a sheltered cove and escaped the wrath of the storm. As soon as the weather cleared the captain and crew left port and it was only by chance that he chose this route to their destination.

The weakened survivors were given water and fed and then the caked salt was washed from them. Their wounds were tended to and each was given clean clothes to replace the tattered rags they were wearing. Sleep would come quickly to them.

Sarah informed the captain that he was now carrying the sultan's daughter. When she told the captain of how these three men from the north had kept them alive the crew was listening and it would be a story retold many times over the next few days. Such is the way legends are born.

The captain ordered some of the crew members to clean his cabin and then turned it over to the women. He found better quarters for the others, amidst the grumblings of crewmembers that were displaced to make some room for their guests. Even the captain bunked with the crew.

This deed would assure him a promotion in the sultans navy and perhaps riches as well. His reward might allow him to buy his own ship and become his own master. The fact that his trade mission was successful wouldn't hurt his chances for promotion either. He could even be appointed a governance somewhere in one of the sultan's provinces.

Now that the survivors were fed, rested and cleaned up their condition improved rapidly. It would take two or three days to reach their destination and they all took some exercise on the deck. The princess accompanied them but had to be supported by Jamie and Liam and she couldn't stay at it very long as it tired her out quickly she was still very weak.

While on deck one night she started to ask Jamie questions.

"Why would a slave save our lives?" she asked, "We are nothing to you."

Jamie was startled by the question and replied, "First let's get one thing straight, we are not slaves, we were knocked unconscious, kidnapped, and chained to an oar by pirates."

"In our countries we are princes. The second thing you need to know is that among my people we try and help women in trouble and we don't ask whether they are common or noble, we just help them."

How strange this man is, she thought to herself, her own countrymen would have stripped her of her jewellery and let the sharks have her, or saved her to demand ransom from the sultan. "Is that what you are after, a ransom?" Aza asked.

Jamie's face turned red and he turned and walked away from her. He was infuriated that she would make such a comment.

She met him on deck later in the evening and apologised to him. Talking to him she learned of their marriage customs and was fascinated to learn that they could pick their own mates.

All of the marriages in her country were arranged and many people were promised in marriage before they were born. All of her friends in court were promised or already married, some to corpulent old men. She was lucky she was marrying a handsome prince. At least she had that. The more the princess got to know Jamie and the others the more she liked them. Her only problem was that she found herself enjoying Jamie's company a little too much.

Sarah found herself in the same dilemma. She had been spending a lot of time with Liam and it astonished her at how well he could speak to her in her own language. To Sarah this longhaired, red-bearded young man was the handsomest man she had ever met. He didn't talk very much and seemed distant at times, why she didn't know.

For these two young girls meeting these men was like a breath of fresh air. Their stories stirred the girls' hearts, inspired them with passion, and fired their imaginations. It was an exhilarating feeling, and when it came upon them remembering their stations became a difficult thing to do.

Jamie's only problem when talking to Aza was the master slave look she always gave him. This was something that had always bothered him because it was a look that all nobles and statesmen seemed to cultivate. Although he was raised as a noble as a child his father had always told him to look right into a man's eyes like he was your equal. He would question her about it.

Later on deck he asked Aza, "Why do you always tilt your head and go stiff when you talk to me? I am not a slave. When you want to talk to me just look me in the eye and say what you want to say."

"Slaves never speak to me the way you do, and in my country you would probably be flogged for doing so." She didn't really know how to answer him, as nobody had ever spoken to her like that before, not even her father. Becoming angry and confused by his words, she returned to her cabin but couldn't stop herself from constantly thinking about this wild, blue-eyed Scotsman.

Jamie thought of her constantly as well and these thoughts disturbed his sleep and appetite as much as hers did.

While on deck the next morning the princess asked him, "What would you do if you were free now?"

"I would return to Scotland with all haste," he replied.

"What would you do when you got there?" she asked. "You have no army, no wealth and no support. You don't even own a sword."

It was Jamie's turn to get angry now and when he did those steel blue eyes would change to a grey green colour that would shine with a sparkle and pierce your soul, if you had one.

"I will find a way back to my island even if I have to swim back, princess," he said. "I must reclaim my throne and avenge the dishonour done to my family, if I have any left. Nothing on this earth will stop me from reaching this goal." He then returned to his small cabin in a fine temper.

How different these people are, she thought to herself. These people seem to have the courage to face anything head on with little regard to their own fate or consequence. Where do these qualities come from? She wondered.

In another day they would land on her father's dock with all that had happened she had forgot how much she missed him. Soon thoughts of her new husband and marriage would occupy her time.

Once docked, they were loaded on a wagon and driven to the palace.

Liam had been sick for a couple of days and had to be carried onto the wagon.

While riding to the palace Aza couldn't help but steal furtive glances at Jamie and he responded in kind. The sultan had been given the news that his daughter had arrived by messenger. After hearing the tales of the storm's fury from his aides, he had given up all hope of ever seeing her again.

He anxiously awaited them for now his throne might yet have an heir, and the threat of war was diminished.

For Jamie and the others the end of the voyage presented a new set of circumstances and an unknown fate.

Now that they had landed, Jamie wondered where their destiny would take them. He and his cousins had survived as galley slaves and they had survived an ocean voyage few could imagine. It was a miracle that any of them were alive.

Jamie was also aware that he had fallen in love with a woman that had been promised to another and he was greatly disturbed about it. Being in a strange land with strange customs would be another challenge they would have to face.

One more concern of was, how would they get home? He thought that the boast he made to the princess could be an empty and hollow boast. Aza was right about one thing; they had nothing to return with or the means to accomplish anything at the moment. This was a problem they would have to overcome at any cost. Their futures depended on it.

Little did James Cameron realise that destiny and fate were about to change their lives forever. In time all of their questions would be answered. For now they must wait anxiously and hope that chance favours them.

THE NEW KING

"Your plans are complete, my lord," stated William Cameron's lieutenant, Ian Strathcon.

In this life he was a brigand, bullyboy, thief and assassin. In fact any dirty deed that needed to be done usually had his hand in it. This vile creature was William's right hand man and enforcer. He and William had been friends for many years now. This friendship was now starting to pay off and he was very happy about this.

"My brother is dead, and his heirs are also dead?" the king enquired.

"Yes, my lord, those that aren't dead are on their way to a different kind of death," Ian replied with a laugh in his voice.

"And what of my sister-in-law, Fiona, she is well, and no worse for wear I hope?" he said with a smile.

"No, my lord," Ian replied with a slight sneer on his face for he knew what his master had in store for her tonight. William had been infatuated with her beauty from the first moment he met her. That she belonged to his brother John didn't matter to him in the least, for he knew one day he would possess her and today was that day.

Fiona was the most beautiful woman he had ever seen and, her beauty soon possessed his mind and he soon began to plot to take over all of his brother's possessions including his wife. The madness would eventually consume him.

William began to build up alliances shortly after John brought Fiona over from Ireland. Most of his alliances were with Norse-Irish outlaws, fugitives and renegade Norseman. William used any manner of dealing to achieve his goal; from blackmail, outright theft, or murder, it didn't matter. He would get his throne and queen regardless of the cost in lives or gold. In these times men were bought as cheaply as livestock, and William was assembling a large group of thieves and cutthroats, which he quickly turned into an elite group of fast mobile cavalry.

This group of raiders went up and down the coast of both islands spreading fear and terror among the residents. This group robbed and raided with impunity in some areas. William started to build up his fortune in this manner, as well as doing legitimate deals to solidify his position.

***

The chamber was pleasant enough, but to be brought here at sword point was something new for the wife of a king. It was an experience she didn't want to repeat. She knew her husband was dead, the fate of her children she didn't know. One of the maidservants informed her of John's death and she was very proud when she heard that several of the traitors had paid with their lives by John's sword before he was finally cut down. She loved him dearly and would miss his touch. With him she had never felt more loved.

Fiona didn't know what had happened as when John rushed off to see what the problem was, he had her escorted to safety away from her chamber. She supposed by his order, but thinking back she realised it was that filth that called himself William's friend who had escorted her to the chamber. What was he doing here? She asked herself, something wasn't right. What was this all about?

A queen as always, she faced her fate with as much calm as she could muster. Being the wife of a king had given her the fortitude to withstand the lying, gossip, and other petty jealousies of court life but this was something different and she didn't like the feeling she was getting. Things had changed.

Was she still a queen...? Fiona wondered, and soon her fears began to manifest. These manifestations were laid bare when a drunken, filthy, blood-spattered William strode into her chamber and gazed upon his new trophy. He stood swaying in the doorway as he drank in the beauty of her form and the fullness of her lips, they would be his tonight.

"Won't you even offer your new king and lord a chair?" he bellowed.

"My new king... what do you want, William? I don't have time to play games, I have to find out what has become of my family."

"Don't worry, you have lots of time, and your family has been well taken care of," he reassured her.

"What do you mean?" Fiona asked. "What have you done, William?" she asked.

"Most of your family are already dead, put to the sword by me, or one of my comrades, and now you belong to me," William responded, with a smile on his face like he was enjoying her torment. "After a suitable time of mourning you will be wed to me, and you will further provide me with a couple of heirs to my throne. I know you are still able to bear children and two is a small number, don't you agree?"

"You must be mad, William!" she screamed at him. "You killed my husband, your own brother to lay claim to everything he possessed for your own gains. Is that what this is all about?" Her anger was mounting, to have her husband murdered by an ambitious brother was more than she could take and she lunged at William with a dagger she had concealed beneath her cloak.

William was nearly sliced open because of it.

William was a seasoned warrior and even drunk his reflexes allowed him to block her thrust, and roughly pin her to the bed where he then proceeded to ravage her for the next four hours.

All manner of indignities were forced upon her until the last of her strength was gone and she lay bleeding and sobbing in pain.

His lust sated for the moment, he dressed and headed for the wine cellar, laughing and babbling to himself along the way. Before leaving her company, he turned in the doorway and said, "Unless you want it this way every time, I suggest you show a little more passion my next visit."

William did not return that night for while in search of wine, the wine he had already consumed got the better of him and he passed out on the wine cellar floor waking up many hours later.

Fiona lay on the bed for quite some time before calling for her maidservant who was horrified at the sight she now witnessed, and with good reason.

The reflection of Fiona's face and body in the mirror validated the pain she was feeling. Her lips were split in several places and bleeding, clumps of hair were torn out, two of her teeth were loose, and her face was battered and bruised. Bruised or not, she knew that she would not be able to bear this kind of treatment for long. She had several wounds and bruises on her body as well.

While Fiona's maidservant cleaned and attended her wounds, she made up her mind that she was not going to play William's game, she would soon end this nightmare, and William would pay for his brutality this night.

William had restricted her movements through the castle, but her servants were free to come and go as they pleased. Giving a small bag of coins to her maidservant she instructed her to take it and her message to Riley the castle woodcutter and for him to find her Uncle Donal the Druid priest, and for Donal to come as quickly as he could, for she needed his help. Fiona couldn't do what she planned without his help.

Although Christianity had come to the islands many people still clung to the old values and traditions. The druids were a very wise and learned sect, and they still commanded a fair amount of respect from the common people. Or was it fear?

It had taken many weeks to track down Donal for he travelled widely, and many were suspicious of strangers asking questions. In some parts of the land they were still persecuted and hunted down. This only forced the Druids to travel to spread their teachings and customs on a smaller scale in smaller villages.

William was still away solidifying his new kingdom and would not return for many weeks. It would take that long for Fiona to heal. When she saw Donal she could hardly contain herself, this was the first family member she had made contact with since her ordeal began. He was glad to see her as well; his travels had taken him far. Quickly he told her all that he knew. She was gladdened when he told her that Jamie was alive, although sold into slavery, and two of her daughters were still alive.

Thank God, she prayed silently to herself.

Donal was not so pleased with the news of Jamie for he knew that very few men ever survived where they were going. He dared not tell Fiona for fear of marring her hopes that Jamie would return to claim his throne and restore the kingdom to its former glory.

Once Donal found out why Fiona summoned him, he was angry. "No, my dear, I cannot do what you ask, it is against our ways to do this thing as a sacrifice to the gods, or in battle, or as an act of mercy would be fine. What you ask me to do is murder and I will have no part of it."

"If you don't help me, Donal, I will find another way, of that you can be sure. I cannot live with this shame, and I will never bear children for that animal!" Fiona said angrily. "When my husband ruled his small kingdom he gave refuge to members of your sect when they were being hunted and persecuted, he treated you fairly as well."

The priest wasn't sure if the trauma her experiences in the last few days had unhinged her mind. He had witnessed that before. Her once beautiful face was battered and heavily bruised and he could see she was bruised on the inside as well. To have her husband killed, her family destroyed, and then to be ravished and beaten by a man she called family, was a difficult burden to bear.

It was true that his sect owed much to John, he gave them aid and comfort when needed and never bothered them, even though he was a Christian. The druids had an extensive knowledge of medicine and herbs, but Donal would not use them for this purpose and flatly denied Fiona's request.

Seeing that she could not change his mind, she bid him to leave. Fiona would find another way, she thought to herself.

Fiona decided that the best time to do this would be on her wedding night. This would deny William his victory over her, and cause him much embarrassment as well. Fiona now only had to gather the means for her demise, this she did by sending her maidservant to fetch the ingredients separately. Later she would mix them together for her fatal cocktail. Fiona had time to heal and prepare before William's return, as it would be many weeks before he repaired the damage to his new kingdom, rounded up any traitors and gathered his plunder.

Under Keltic law she knew a meeting of the barons would be called and a new king chosen. William's gold would see to it that his way to the throne was a smooth transition, with no objections, or fuss. After the ceremony to crown William was complete, there would be feasting, which would last for several days. Once completed, he would be free to announce his wedding.

During the next month, in between clashes amongst the clans surrounding his kingdom, he would return and it was always the same, he would violently ravage her and then leave. He no longer beat her, as he wanted to enjoy her beauty as well. His lust was intense; she ached all over each time he would visit. The smell of sweat from his unwashed, unkempt body would linger in her nostrils for days. She could not take much more of this. William's attacks on her body had taken their toll. She was sure something was damaged inside of her.

Fiona didn't want to die before she gave her forthcoming husband a wedding present he would never forget. For the moment she would be more co-operative, eat better, and try and get more exercise and fresh air. She hoped that this would help to keep her going long enough to deliver the final blow to his ego.

How she wished she could see it … the look in those cold dead eyes when she gasped her last breaths in front of him. To be cheated out of his prize on the night of his wedding would drive him mad … or madder than he already was.

The priests were right, she told herself, and our Keltic belief that we will return in another form is now somewhat appealing considering my alternative choice, she mused. I will be reborn and my son will return to wield the sword that my husband cannot and reclaim what is rightfully his. Like all mothers, she wondered what the fate of all her children would be. Would she ever see her two daughters again, and who else amongst her family had felt the edge of William's sword at their throats?

Requiring an hour or two to get ready for her wedding, she assembled all of the ingredients for the toxic potion from the places she had hidden them. Runners would soon bring news of William's approach, she would not disappoint him, and he would soon be wed to the loveliest corpse in Scotland.

William's guests had arrived and Fiona quickly dressed in a beautiful green-blue peacock gown, and put on her finest jewellery. After attending to the myriad details that go with any wedding, she was now ready for him.

Quickly she drank the poison knowing it would take a while to work through her system, she could hear him coming down the hallway. Bursting through the doorway he stopped, mesmerised by her beauty, and already drunk. Slowly the poison started to kick in and she began to slide off her seat.

Trying to hold off his anger and bewildered, he understood what she had done, and he raced to her side only to hear words that would haunt him for years. Feebly Fiona said, "You will not have me any more, false king, and I will provide you with no bastard heirs. I hope you rot in hell!" The shock of what he had just witnessed caused William's brain to short circuit and he went into a tirade of screaming and cursing.

Pacing up and down and screaming at the top of his lungs, William picked up the head of her lifeless body and screamed at her. "You rotten bitch, I still have two of your daughters so one shall be my queen, perhaps I shall breed them both and start a new dynasty." He then dropped her on the cold floor and went staggering off towards the wine cellar.

William's words were wasted on Fiona as she had slipped into oblivion long before he began to rant. Now he would have to turn his cruelty towards something else, and he would.

A servant came nervously to William now drunk and lost in thought, and asked if he should send the guests home. The servant repeated himself several times to a dazed and stupefied William.

"Guests? Wedding? What...? No of course not," he said after regaining his senses. "I will make an announcement at the ceremony."

After the servant left, William wondered how he could use this to his advantage, and came to the conclusion that the queen would die while under the physician's care giving him a believable alibi and a free hand to marry Fiona's daughter when she came of age. This would also give him another blood tie to the throne. The servants that would clean up and remove Fiona's body would have to be killed in order to keep the secret. This didn't bother William in the least.

Finally showing up at the ceremony, he called his guests. "My friends, I know you came here tonight for a wedding and a feast, I am sorry to say there will be no wedding but there will be a feast. The queen has come down with an illness and the physicians have sent her away for treatment. Let us drink up and enjoy, consider the wedding postponed."

Calling on Strathcon he explained what had happened and what was to be done with the servants. Ian left the celebration to carry out his king's wishes and returned a short time later nodding his head to William to acknowledge that the deed was accomplished. William was happy again.

The next morning William awoke with a ferocious hangover and summoned all of the castle servants to him. He wanted to know who had come and gone from the castle during his absence. Even in his drunken stupor his curiosity got the better of him wondering where Fiona had obtained the poison or the ingredients to concoct a poison.

One very nervous servant spoke up and told William that the queen had several visitors that never stayed very long. She had recognised one of them as Donal the druid priest, he had come several times and always left with a foul look on his face, she said.

"Very well you may all go back to your duties. I have, I think, all the information I need for now." Turning to the captain of his guards he asked him if he knew Donal the priest.

The captain told him that he did. "I also know where to find him if needed," he responded.

"Splendid, bring him in, I wish to ask him some questions."

The captain turned and quickly left the room.

William's twisted mind always on the lookout for new ways to turn things to his advantage decided that the Druids were too well respected to be taken lightly. He would have to confer with Ian on a way to dispose of this group in a permanent manner that wouldn't arouse the whole country into armed rebellion.

Donal and his fellow priests were accused of poisoning the queen, and thus subject to the king's justice.

It would be a swift and brutal justice to be sure.

Two hours later the captain returned with Donal the priest. William was summoned and immediately began to question Donal. "You have been coming to the castle quite a lot the last couple of weeks, is this not so priest?" the king asked.

"Yes, my lord," Donal responded. "The work of a priest is never done and many are in need of comfort these days."

William didn't miss the sarcasm in his remarks. "The queen has been poisoned and I'm at a loss to figure out where she would get the knowledge to concoct a poison. Almost immediately I thought of you, strange isn't it?"

Donal was questioned for some time and knew that William had already made up his mind that Donal was guilty. Donal tried to explain that as his niece she had been given herbal knowledge at a young age as were many. Figuring he was already dead anyway, he then went on and tried to tell the king that the taxes he had imposed and the other injustices were causing restlessness among the people.

"I do not care what you priests or the peasants want. I rule this kingdom not them!" William roared. "Drag this trash out of this chamber and throw him in the dungeon!"

The captain looked at William and hesitated for a moment before asking, "Do you think that is wise, my lord, the druids are still a powerful sect with a long reach." The guard was hesitant for he had attended several druid rituals and was a little fearful of their power. It was a different kind of power than William's, and one he couldn't explain.

William was getting agitated. "Do as I tell you or you will feel my sword point along with any of your men that may share your concerns. Now go and do what you're told!" The guard left shaking his head.

The king is losing his mind, he said to himself and I will have to keep a closer eye on him and see where this goes.

The captain turned Donal over to the other guards to lock up and informed them of the king's threat against them. They were not impressed.

The king's birthday came and an impressive banquet was held in his honour and the crowd was in a festive mood for William was lining their pockets with gold, life was good.

The trumpets sounded upon William's arrival and he signalled to the musicians to halt their playing. He would be speaking to an already intoxicated crowd.

"My lords, thanks to our conquests and expansions, and with the help of our Norse brothers, we now control most of the north of Scotland, and I believe a new era of prosperity awaits us." He was answered by cheering and a lot of boisterous yelling.

William nodded to the musicians to resume playing. William had paid tribute to the Norsemen for they kept the king's trade routes open, and kept the waterways free from piracy. He did not trust then and knew that once his gold supply ran out they probably would turn on him. For now everyone was happy and drunk.

The feasting and revelry went on till the wee hours in the morning and after most of his guests had passed out, William staggered to his chamber. His brain was fogged and the serving wench he had taken to his bed gave him little comfort, he wanted his queen. Damn her, he thought to himself, screaming at the girl to get out. He then passed out on his bed not waking until late in the afternoon.

William awoke in a foul mood and the noise from the workmen at the castle added to his discomfort. He had ordered plans for an expansion of the castle to nearly five times its present size. Having enough gold to buy all the loyalty he needed, and the workmen to expand the castle pleased him immensely. Things were going better than he planned.

It was a damp and grey afternoon that greeted William. He half staggered down to the dungeon to question Donal once more. Finding the jailer asleep, he roused him awake and ordered him to open the cell door.

Donal quickly got to his feet after William had entered and for a few moments stood eyeing each other. Donal was nearly the same size and build as William. He had been a skilled warrior in his day, he didn't fear him.

William stepped back and asked Donal why he killed his queen, a charge he flatly denied.

"Have you gone completely mad, William? Why would I want to kill my niece? I helped raise her as a child?" It was the wrong thing to say to William. Donal tried to explain to William that Fiona had asked him to teach her more herbal knowledge as she wished to become a healer. He didn't know that she would use this knowledge for the purpose that she did.

William wasn't listening. "You are a liar, priest, and it's time you paid for those lies!" William screamed. Reaching over he grabbed the guard's sword and plunged it into Donal's chest. "Say hello to my queen when you see her, as you will now be joining her in the afterlife!" William taunted him.

Falling to the ground with blood spurting out of his chest, Donal cursed William and told him that one day he would pay for this treachery, and all his gold wouldn't change that. He then departed this world cursing William's name.

William kicked the body over and walked out of the cell, ordering the jailer to have the body taken out and tossed into the castle moat as a warning to others.

"I'll pay, will I?" William babbled to himself. "I guess today isn't that day, priest." Then he left the dungeon.

The jailer did as he was told, but with ill feeling. This sensation got the better of him and he decided to grab his cloak and flee this place. Thinking William mad, he didn't want to be around when the Druids found out one of their own had been tossed out like garbage and thrown into a moat. These priests had a fearful kind of power, and the jailer knew if they found out he had done this terrible thing, his own life would be in jeopardy, and this he would not risk.

THE PERSIAN KING

The three young men, and they were men now, the boy being lost forever to the lash and whip, had grown considerably over the last three years. Each man now carried a magnificently sculptured body and each stood well over six feet tall. Wolf was nearly six feet eight inches, and weighed in at around two hundred and eighty-five pounds of rock solid muscle.

As these three young men were being led through the courtyards to the palace they stood in awe of the amount of wealth lavished on the palace decoration. They passed gold and bronze statues, rich mosaic work, carved ivory statues, jewel encrusted objects of art, silk tapestries, and lush hanging gardens.

"Have you ever seen anything like this before?" Wolf said. "I have never seen this amount of wealth, and indeed didn't know there was this kind of wealth in any land."

"Aye," Liam responded. "I don't think there is this wealth of gold and jewels in all of the British Isles, or the continent."

The air was dry in this country and the warm breezes carried the mingled exotic scents of spices, flowers and perfumes to them. They passed the sultan's private zoo that housed many exotic and strange animals they had never seen before, or had even imagined.

Each man wondered what fate had in store for them. Would they be sent back to a galley? Would they be executed? Or thrown into a dungeon to rot? Down to the large gallery where the sultan held court they marched, still in chains.

All eyes in the sultan's court followed them until they were brought before the sultan. They were still in chains because the sultan and his advisors were not sure if their story was true or not.

"Step forward," the sultan commanded, and each moved forward. "I understand that you speak our language, so I will dispense with any formal introductions for now. I have only one question, why do three galley slaves save the life of a princess and her maidservant? Did you think there would be a reward? How much is it you want?"

The three looked at each other bewildered. It was James that spoke up first.

"First of all, your Highness, we are not slaves, yours or anyone else's. At the time nobody was thinking about any reward, only survival, and we didn't know she was a princess until she regained consciousness. In our country we try and help men and women in distress, it is our way."

The courtyard palace was buzzing, not in many years had they heard anyone talk to the sultan in that manner or tone.

A few cried out. "How dare they! Who are these upstarts? Return them to the galley! What impudence!" they shouted.

"Silence!" the sultan roared. He then sat back on this throne and thought over what James had asked. "Who is it that did this to you?"

"We were knocked unconscious, kidnapped and sold as slaves to one of your pirate galleys by an uncle who claimed my father's and Liam's father's kingdom as his own. We know little else about it."

Wolf spoke next. "Your Highness, the conspiracy involving our families had been planned for some time, why they seized our father's kingdom we do not know. Our father's lands were not rich as far as we know and our people seemed contented."

"You are from the cold lands to the north of here where men wear the skins of animals, is this not so?" the sultan asked.

"Yes, your Highness. I am from a land called Danemark and my people are often called Vikings. And yes it is cold there. We are a seafaring people," he added.

Liam was the next one questioned. "What of the one with the flaming red hair, what land do you come from?"

"I am from Ireland, your Highness… it is a large island not far from where James lives, we are cousins, and his mother and mine are sisters."

"Does your mother have hair such as you? If so, she must be an astonishing woman to gaze upon," the sultan exclaimed.

"She is indeed a beautiful woman and with some luck I intend to see her again if she lives."

"Do you now?" the sultan said with a smile on his face. This one had an intensity about his that's hard to explain. He wondered if these boys were properly trained in the use of arms, what kind of warriors would they turn into? He would speak to Po about this in the morning. As it turned out it was a very wise decision on the sultan's part.

The three young men that stood before him were the most unusual collection of slave-princes he had ever encountered. Sitting silently on his throne for a few moments the sultan rose and faced the court. He declared that these three young men were to be unshackled and given free run of the palace, and their wishes were to be looked after.

Explaining that he would be away for some time to meet the prince, his future son-in-law, to make the arrangements for his daughter's wedding, he added that they were to be treated as his personal guests. Turning to walk back to his chambers, he could only laugh to himself thinking these three have balls the size of elephants, for no one in his court would dare speak to him as these three did.

Above all the sultan valued courage and honour. His sons and beloved wife were killed during the plague that swept the region some years before. Aza was all he had left.

The sultan was an intelligent, resourceful man and he soon thought of a plan involving the boys that might just bring peace to his troubled land. He would send for Po in the morning.

Until the sultan returned these three young men were free to take in the wonders of the palace and the strange and mysterious city that soon began to captivate them. They spent the next several days absorbing the sights and sounds of this unfamiliar world that they were thrust into. It was not an unpleasant place to be for the city and market square offered many diversions and pleasures for young men.

During this waiting period each wondered what was next, would they be killed for speaking back to the sultan? Would they be sent back to the galleys this time as slaves of the sultan? Or would they all die for touching the princess?

"It will probably be me they execute first," Liam stated.

"Why do you say that, Liam?" Jamie asked.

"I was the one that slapped the princess and bandaged her leg, their customs may require it."

Wolf then spoke up and said, "We all know they have strange customs here, but I doubt very much that they would kill us after saving the princess's life unless they are barbarians after all."

"Just the same, I think we should keep our eyes open and our wits about us, our lives rest in the hands of these people for the moment. We have to get through this and go home."

The days and nights of food and drink as well as rest and sleeping with soft covers on their beds had done wonders and they were healing. They were still apprehensive of their fate but felt better to face it together, united as one.

Several days later the sultan returned and proclaimed to his assembled court that in a little over two years' time the prince would come to claim his bride and bring peace between their two nations. The sultan had told the prince of these wild men from the north and their incredible tale of survival and of their insolence in his court. The prince was intrigued by what he heard and was looking forward to meeting them.

The sultan looked resplendent in a black silk robe with large embossed silver dragons shimmering and reflecting light whenever he moved. His six foot two frame, sharply trimmed beard, and piercing black eyes gave him an imposing and almost spectral appearance.

In a voice loud enough to be heard at the farthest end of the royal courtyard he retold the story that most of the courtiers already knew.

"Several weeks ago my daughter was lost at sea and saved from certain death by these three young men. They told me of how they were clubbed, hi-jacked and forced to serve aboard a pirate galley. I have heard the lies and tales of many men in my time but the conviction on their voices tells me their story is true. It is the kind of story I do not like to hear," he said while looking at various members of his court that he knew were disloyal. They got the message.

"From this day forth these three young men are honorary citizens of this nation and my personal guests, should any harm come to them during their stay here, I will consider it a personal insult to me and the offending party will feel my wrath and you will not like it, I assure you."

Sitting back on his throne again the sultan commanded the trio to come closer to him and face him.

"You young men saved the life of my daughter and secured the peace between two countries. Is there anything a grateful father and sultan can grant you for what you have done? It is a miracle that any of you survived. Surely a greater hand not of this earth guides your destiny."

Jamie spoke up. "Your Highness, we do not seek any reward, we ask that you only lend us some swords and provisions that we may return and reclaim our birth rights."

The sultan sat back in disbelief at what he had just heard, I just offered these men anything they wanted and all they ask for is swords and provision, he thought to himself. I must learn more about this race of men. Their lack of greed was like a breath of fresh air to the sultan.

Leaning forward the sultan asked, "Do you know how to use a sword? Have you ever been in battle?"

"We have not skills of battle or use of the sword, but we will learn," Jamie responded.

The sultan now seated, rose and walked towards the three. "Your courage does you well, but it will not stop a battle hardened warrior determined to kill you. You do not have the necessary skills to win battle, but this can be learned. Tomorrow you will begin training with my sword master and you will learn the arts of war."

The whole courtyard was buzzing now for Master Po, a former general in the emperor of China's army was a very deadly swordsman. This was an exceptional honour for only the sultan and his elite bodyguard were trained by Master Po.

The sultan added, "It will not be easy and the training will be hard, but when finished you will be able to use your sword as a warrior should. Do not worry about your teacher, when he first came to me seven swordsmen attacked him in ambush at night and all seven were buried the next day."

Clapping his hands, three large chests were brought in and opened before them. The trio stared in disbelief; each of the chests contained enough gold and jewels to buy a small kingdom. The chests were then locked up and removed.

"When you are ready to reclaim your thrones, this treasure goes with you, for men fight for gold as well as honour and with this you should be able to assemble a formidable army" the sultan said. "It is the least I can do for you."

The trio dazed by their sudden reversal in fortune, thanked the sultan and returned to their quarters.

Signalling to his attendant to dismiss the court the sultan turned and returned to his chambers. The murmuring and chattering continued out in the open courtyard for quite some time as people gathered in small groups to discuss the local gossip and the sultan's proclamations.

The three shocked young men were led back to their rooms by a little servant called Ezra. He explained to them that he was their chaperon and guide when needed. Ezra explained the laws of the land, informed them of proper conduct, and everything they would need to know about getting accustomed to their new Life. This took nearly two hours and then Ezra left.

Back in their rooms the cousins couldn't believe their good fortune for now they had the means to accomplish their goal and return home,

Liam spoke up and said, "I can't believe this is really happening, for the first time I really think we can get back our kingdoms."

"Aye," Wolf said. "Paying those bastards back that did this to our families is going to be a pleasure, and I too feel that we can really do this now."

"Just the same, we better keep our eyes and ears open around here for I don't know how much we can trust the people of this land," Jamie said.

"I agree," Liam said. "While we were in court I noticed groups of people that didn't seem too happy with what the sultan told them, there may be treachery afoot."

"I don't know how either of you saw anything as you couldn't seem to take your eyes off the women in the court," Wolf said. They all laughed.

"Just the same," Wolf added, "we had better be careful around the princess and her servants. I don't think these people put up with people messing around with their women. Have you noticed that most of their women wear veils? If we aren't careful we might lose our heads."

Liam answered him by saying: "Well if you lost your head we wouldn't have to look at your ugly face any more, perhaps you should consider wearing a veil." Laughing, this comment soon started a free for all wrestling match between the young princes, as often happened with them, it was a friendly contest with Wolf usually emerging the victor.

Master Po watched from the balcony and thought to himself, it looks as though I finally have some worthy pupils to teach. Po saw qualities in these three that were lacking in most of his pupils.

All three soon learned the training was hard, they learned the arts of war quickly under the tutelage of Master Po.

From Po's teachings they learned of wars and battles fought in far off lands, and of kings and battles from a forgotten time. They learned the secrets of war and tactics from an ancient general known as Sun Tzu. They absorbed these lessons willingly and without question.

Master Po taught them philosophy and a better than average knowledge of battlefield medicine, as well as chuan-fa (unarmed combat), horsemanship, archery, and the use of spear and sword.

He conditioned then to fall and roll in one motion return returning to a combat stance ready to continue the fight. The training sessions were long and hard and they learned fast and adapted to each new situation and tactic as a seasoned warrior would.

During their training with the sword they learned the butterfly and swallowtail sword techniques and a host of other martial skills they would need. Liam particularly enjoyed the two-handed sword technique. These lessons were constantly repeated until they became natural reflexes.

The boys had grown into men and the men were becoming skilled warriors, it would soon be time to try out all that they learned. One thing Jamie had learned from his studies was that men followed courage, even if it meant their own undoing. This was a dangerous path to follow.

One evening after a particularly hard training session, Jamie sat thinking about what 'kingship' meant. To him kingship meant an inspiring leader, who made wise decisions and treated men justly. He hoped he could become this kind of leader. Little did he know that he already was.

The years that had gone by since their capture nearly five years ago had given the conspirators time to build up forces, solidify their positions, and dig in.

Jamie was also thinking about home and wondered if the memory of them had left their families, or indeed if they had any family left at all.

Knowing they would have to leave Master Po bothered him as well for Po had become like a father figure to them. He was their teacher but he had also become a friend. Unbeknown to these young men Master Po considered them like his own sons.

Po's sons were murdered by members of the emperor's imperial guard many years ago while he was off soldiering in some distant land. The guards who murdered his sons did not live long, and it was the main reason he resided in Persia.

Both Po and Jamie did have one concern they both shared and that was Liam. Since his brother had been killed aboard the pirate ship he had become withdrawn and sullen. The fun loving part of him was gone. He seemed to possess an inner rage that would come and go with terrible ferocity. It was like an ethereal glow would surround him at these times.

During the many months of training Jamie would often get up during the night and find Liam out in the courtyard practising a new sword technique for hours. He trained harder than Wolf or Jamie and was becoming a very deadly swordsman.

When making their rounds the palace guard wouldn't even bother him. They respected his skill with a sword partly out of fear. These were dangerous times.

FORBIDDEN LOVE AND OTHER ADVENTURES

There was no doubt of it, Jamie was madly in love with Aza, and she was with him. They had a big problem ... trying to share that love in a palace full of traitors, spies, and gossips. As the sultan's only daughter she was watched over.

Aza's marriage was a long way off and for most of the trio's stay she lived much as she had before their arrival. They had many things to learn from one another. She knew her father liked them; he was impressed when they spoke up in court.

Often she would watch them training and found herself getting excited and warm all over as she watched their muscled bodies sweating, while they performed their exercises. Sarah would accompany her and she had the same feelings as Aza, only her eyes were for Liam only. Sarah still couldn't get much out of Liam; he was moody, sullen, and quiet. He was getting more comfortable with her but it was a slow process.

The princess knew her father well, and if he let them have the run of the palace, it was for a good reason. The sultan had no sons so perhaps it filled a void in his life. Knowing her father as well as she did, she also figured he had some grand scheme planned for them. He was an exceptional chess player.

Jamie, like all men in love, couldn't get the princess off his mind for even a moment and some days it even affected his training. On these days he would often find himself playing chess with the sultan.

The sultan knew why Jamie showed up at his chamber door on these nights. They played chess and talked of many things, often long into the night. Both contestants learned much from each other.

Sometimes it was what they talked about and the way they talked of things. The sultan enjoyed his company, and Liam's as well. Wolf wasn't much of a chess player although he did have an occasional match with the sultan.

Their lives were enriched by these talks and as his daughter had surmised he had plans for these three. There were few in court that he could trust and he felt a real kinship with Jamie and his cousins. The sultan knew he would have to play his game carefully and not overplay or he could lose all. He would have to watch and make sure that things didn't go too far with Jamie and Aza.

After a period of time Aza was allowed to ride with Jamie and a small escort. They were ordered to keep a reasonable distance between them as Aza wanted time alone with Jamie. Often they would ride to some of the larger oases and picnic and swim. She loved to watch Jamie swim in the cool waters. He offered to teach her to swim but she declined.

Sarah and Liam often accompanied them on these excursions and having her along no doubt convinced the court that Aza's motives were pure. Unfortunately they were wrong, when four young people are in love the lines between duty and honour become rather blurred. Aza treated Sarah more like a friend than a servant and always had so their secrets were safe with each other.

She was fascinated by Liam's quiet demeanour and brooding ways. After he finally broke down and told her why he was often so bitter, she understood and it just made her love him more. Their love for each other could be openly shown as Sarah was a servant and not a princess while Aza and Jamie's love was forbidden.

Although their relationship was condoned Liam was looked down upon by some of the court for being a love between a commoner and a prince. None would dare say anything openly to him lest they end up on the point of his sword. Liam's skill with a sword was well known in court.

A court member had made the mistake of confronting Liam shortly after his arrival over some trivial matter and the man harboured ill feeling towards him. While in the market square just minding his own business admiring some of the craftsmen's wares he was confronted by his adversary and two of his drunken friends.

Liam seldom went out alone and never would again after this day. He tried to avoid this fight but he was cornered in an alley by three assailants. Following Po's advice when outnumbered, attack, and so he did.

Taken by surprise, he quickly dispatched one of his attackers and cut the sword arm of another very badly. Now down to two assailants, it was only a matter of time before the one bleeding profusely would slow down and collapse, and he did. The only one left was the man Liam had his initial confrontation with and seeing his partner collapse he rushed between them to finish Liam off and made a thrust that Liam was barely able to avoid.

The third man was alone now and pressed his attack on a bloody and tired Liam who had sustained several large sword cuts during the battle. Tripping as his assailant pressed him Liam fell to the floor and as his opponent raised his sword to deliver the killing blow, Liam rolled out and drove his dagger into the stomach of his stunned attacker.

Dropping his sword and clutching his stomach in disbelief Liam's assailant fell backwards as the life drained from him. Liam was near collapse himself and as he fell to the ground a soldier from the palace guard caught him and returned him to the palace.

Those who witnessed the battle quickly spread the news of Liam's victory and another chapter of this young prince's life was written. This was a costly chapter as Liam was badly wounded.

The physicians were summoned and under the watchful eye of Master Po, Liam's wounds were bandaged and cleaned. He had lost a lot of blood and was badly cut in several places. Po worried and ordered a guard to stand at Liam's chamber and watch him.

Liam did have one thing going for him, and that was Sarah, she never left his side and watched over him like a mother hen guarding her chicks. After a few days of rest, Liam began to come around and Jamie and Wolf came to see him on a regular basis. Another constant visitor was Kasim, the captain of the palace archers.

"Liam, you're looking better today, soon you will be able to return to your training instead of loafing about having a pretty nurse waiting on you hand and foot," he said with a smile.

Trying to laugh without breaking open his wounds, Liam replied, "Well the good news, Kasim, is that even before the fight I was better looking than any of the fat, overfed, members of the Royal Archers."

Kasim quickly slid over to Liam with an angry look on his face that quickly changed to a smile as he bent over to kiss him on both cheeks and then embraced him. Liam always hated this custom and Kasim knew it. They both laughed for a few minutes.

These two had been friends since Liam's arrival, as Liam was a fair archer and this impressed Kasim. During their stay with the sultan there would be many nights of adventures enjoying all that palace and city life could provide.

Even though the young men relentlessly teased their new friends about their looks, they were indeed a handsome group of friends. In fact Rizhad and Kasim never seemed to have much trouble winning the hands of fair ladies.

Jamie was head over heels in love with a woman that he could never have and he didn't know what to do about it. He was in a strange land with strange customs and the thought that he would have to leave one day tormented him daily.

Aza would show the trio around the palace as well as giving them guided tours of some or the ancient palaces and temples, long since abandoned. Rizhad and a small group of armed men usually accompanied them, as there were armed villains and thieves roaming through the land. Much of the land was difficult to patrol and many areas were inhospitable.

A group of these bandits decided to attack their party on one outing and it would be the last party they ever attended.

Jamie and Aza had wandered off, as was their usual custom, and the guards ignored them. The two lovers had found a small outdoor garden and pond at the back of the ruined temple they were camped at. When Aza was in Jamie's arms she never feared anything the desert could throw at her. It often astonished her at how tender, affectionate, and caring this rough, tough, wildman from the north could be.

The first outlaw attacked, but Jamie saw him coming and dispatched him with ease. It was the second and third attackers that worried him; they had crazed looks in their eyes. He ordered Aza to get down under the bench they were sitting on. Jamie didn't want to send her away for fear she might be kidnapped. He wanted her where he could keep an eye on her.

Wolf, Rizhad and Kasim had heard the bandits ride in and were silently and slowly sneaking up on them, silencing many with arrows before attacking them en masse. The bandits thought they had stumbled upon a small caravan and thought it would be an easy time. They were wrong.

Jamie had learned much and when his two attackers charged together he was thrown a little off balance, but recovered quickly and charged them. His opponents were now off balance and before they could recover both were shot down by arrows from Kasim and Wolf's bows.

Rizhad and the rest had attacked from the rear of the main body of the outlaws and it soon became a real melee. Jamie now grabbed another sword from one of the fallen bandits and joined the fight swinging both swords through the air like a buzz saw. This was a magnificent sight to see and those that witnessed it were amazed, no one had ever seen Jamie this mad before.

His attacks on the bandits spurred them on and although outnumbered three to one all of the outlaws were killed. In the morning the bodies of forty-seven bandits were heaped in piles everywhere and there were eleven bodies around Jamie.

Only two of their party were killed but nearly all were cut and wounded to some extent. The bandits were stripped of any gold, jewels, and property and then buried. Jamie was asked what they should do with their property and Jamie ordered it distributed among the men. This act gained him another dozen friends.

Rizhad tried to tell Jamie that the men he killed were less than men and if the sultan were here he would have hunted down the bandits that got away and they would have suffered a far worse fate than he meted out to them. Rizhad figured they were attacked by around a hundred outlaws. It was a miracle that they weren't all killed; they were outnumbered three to one.

Jamie just nodded and then left the group returning to his chambers and tried to sleep but this was a fitful sleep at best.

Rizhad watched Jamie leave and he understood and knew he would be alright it would just take some time for now Jamie had to work things out in his own mind. He had experienced the same thing when he first joined the guards. Confronting a thief that had entered the palace one night, they fought a vicious battle that nearly cost Rizhad his life. He understood the cold, hollow, empty feeling that Jamie now felt. He didn't like it either.

Tossing and turning a frantic Jamie headed to Aza's chamber and when she saw the look on his face she ran and threw her arms around him kissing and holding him tightly. He began to sob, she held him for what seemed like hours but wasn't even aware of the time, nor did she care. They knew they had found love and they knew it was a forbidden, but for now they would just hold each other and dream of better days.

The next day Jamie visited the sultan and after they talked he felt more himself. The sultan assured Jamie that he did the right thing, the outlaws were a scourge that needed to be stopped.

After the battle was over, Jamie sat alone by the fire and said little to anyone, brooding alone he wondered if he had gone mad. All he could remember was a roaring red sea of rage in his mind; it was as though fireworks had gone off in his head. This night he scared himself, and it worried him.

Around a different fire in muffled conversation, Wolf told Liam that he had never seen Jamie that angry nor had he ever seen him use a sword like that before.

"Aye," Liam quietly replied, "when I saw him pick up that second sword and attack I thought he was crazy, he even scared me a little. I also know we use two sword techniques but not like he did, he moved like a bronze statue come to life with very disjointed movements, almost in slow motion."

The next morning the battered and bloodied group rode for the palace. Even the princess kept her distance from Jamie, she was a little frightened of what she witnessed this day. The ride back to the palace seemed to take forever. Their wounds were bandaged and they were bathed and fed. They would then sleep through the day and gather in the evening for dinner, enjoying the cool breezes of the desert night.

It was a sullen and morose Jamie that joined the group this evening. He had never enjoyed taking a man's life and it bothered him greatly. He dreamed of the day when he could return home and hopefully rule a peaceful kingdom.

This was another lesson young James Cameron would learn on his road to kingship, it was a long hard road and unforgiving.

After tossing and turning for over an hour, Jamie dressed and headed for Aza's chamber. When she saw him and the look on his face she ran and threw her arms around him. After a lengthy kiss and embrace, Jamie laid his head on her shoulders and began to sob. He stayed there the rest of the night. They knew they had found love, it was a forbidden love and it had no future but for now they just revelled in each other's company.

The next day Jamie felt better and more like himself and visited the sultan who knew the story of their adventure and assured Jamie that he did the right thing, the outlaws were a scourge and he offered to reward him which Jamie turned down.

Jamie next visited Rizhad and it was he that suggested the next trip be a lion or boar hunt and they would leave all the women behind. Jamie agreed and three weeks later the trio and their new friends set off to hunt lion.

They would hunt from chariots and the young princes were both excited and curious never having hunted like this before. As always with this group, there was as much betting and racing along the way. The hunting grounds were about two days ride from the palace and upon reaching them they began a more cautious approach, they were in dangerous territory now.

Some of the prides that inhabited the region contained as many as forty to fifty lions in their families. The hunting grounds were a series of low lying rounded rock formations that looked as though they had been planted, sprouted and then collapsed. These formations were strewn with cool dark caves that the desert lions called home.

Kasim was approaching a large black-maned lion that had been sunning itself on a flat rocky outcrop when another leapt at him from above. The lion knocked both him and his driver into the sand and then turned ready to charge at them. By then Kasim had an arrow fitted and as the lion came leaping at them he was stopped in mid-air as Kasim's arrow pierced the lion's heart.

The momentum of the charging lion knocked them once more onto the sand as well as upsetting the chariot. Quickly righting the chariot they continued on and by the end of the day's hunt eleven lions had been bagged. Jamie was impressed; the lions were worthy adversaries, and fierce quarry worthy of the hunt. They would go again in the future.

Wolf and Liam were also impressed as they had never seen or hunted lions before arriving in this land. They had each bagged a lion and were very proud of this accomplishment. Jamie was beginning to enjoy his stay here and he admired the Persians. They were a rough wild people but at the same time their civilization was very refined. Their culture produced great thinkers, poets and astrologers, and men of science. Skilled architects and artisans built and embellished their palaces and temples.

Jamie and Aza's visits became so frequent that the chaperones and guards didn't even pay attention to them anymore. The future king tried to suppress his feelings for the princess but couldn't as everything had become meshed together and the more he fought the emotion the worse his desire for her became.

Aza never left his thoughts, and began to affect his moods.

Things were no different for the princess, it was true she had loved her future husband as a child but the love she felt for Jamie was new and powerful, and she had never felt like this before. The circumstances of each of their lives made sure that this could never be a permanent love and this upset the princess greatly. She now wished that her father did have a son or sons, as she would be free of her obligations.

One night as the two lovers were gazing at the stars and dreaming of things they could never have, Jamie startled the princess by telling her that they should stop spending so much time together.

"Why?" she asked. "Have I done something to displease you?"

"No nothing like that," Jamie responded, "we both have obligations to our families. I wish we didn't." Jamie rose up from the bench they were seated at sharply, and pounded his fists against the mosaiced wall cursing as he did so; she saw the fire in his eyes and the flush in his cheeks as he paced up and down in front of her. Finally calming down, he sat beside her again and they talked. It was agreed that they would still try and meet in secret and with much more discretion.

This was decided upon as there was already a lot of talk and gossip around the palace and hopefully this would put an end to some of the rumours circulating around the court. It did.

Jamie trained harder and as he made friends along the way he was able to put some distance between the princess and himself.

Jamie's cousins were glad to see the change in him but were still a little apprehensive as they knew they would meet in secret many times over the next years. Even though their love was forbidden and could not be flaunted openly as lovers they would find a way. Liam and Wolf would have to keep their eyes on the two of them, as they didn't want to lose their heads, after surviving what they had so far.

Unfortunately Jamie could not avoid contact with the princess around the palace, and on many occasions like banquets and feasts all they could do was steal furtive glances at one another and hope nobody noticed. Most didn't but the few that did would use this knowledge for their own gains in the future.

Training hard to forget Aza, Jamie's swordsmanship improved to the point where he could match or defeat anyone in the hall. The only two he couldn't beat were Po and Wolf. Wolf usually won his matches by sheer strength and size; he was a very powerful swordsman. During a few training sessions Po was having a hard time keeping Jamie at bay, and although he wouldn't admit it, he was very proud of him.

Many days Jamie would gather one of his companions or even the sultan and they would ride through the desert, often racing for miles. The sultan enjoyed these rides and his affection for these three young princes grew over time. When the desire became too strong in the princess she would visit family members in other provinces for extended periods. It was little comfort.

One evening while riding through the desert on a cool moonlit night, Jamie thought back to the day when Rizhad and some of the others tried to teach them how to ride and race camels.

Liam tried mounting his camel several times and ended up head over heels in the sand. The chorus of laughter did little to instil confidence and after four or five more tries he managed to stay on top his mount.

Jamie didn't fare much better and after being dumped into the sand as his camel raced on into the desert without him he found himself both cursing and laughing along with the rest of his friends. His major humiliation came when the camel returned, sat down in front of him and then spit in his eye. This prompted Jamie to spit in the camel's eye and for the next few minutes the desert witnessed a strange thing as a man and a camel were engaged in a spitting contest.

During all of this, Jamie's friends were of no help for they were rolling on the ground holding their stomachs in pain they were laughing so hard. Wolf was the next victim but to everyone's surprise he mounted and managed to stay on his camel. He almost made it look easy. He only had one problem, Eskandar and Jamshid joined them on this excursion and Jamshid couldn't help having some fun with his old friend.

He decided to partly slice through the straps holding Wolf in his saddle as he knew with Wolf's size and weight it wouldn't take long before he tumbled in the sand. Jamshid didn't want to hurt his friend so he played his trick while the trio were being instructed in the race and its procedures.

Rizhad walked them around the course slowly giving the trio some time to get the feel for their animals and when they returned to the position they started from he lined them up for a quick race. Jamshid would drop the starting flag and Eskandar would flag the finish.

The race started well, but in the second turn Wolf's harness came apart and his camel stopped dead in the sand, sending Wolf flying over its head, narrowly missing being plunged head first into the arse of Liam's camel that had just crossed in front of him. He was lucky this was only a slow warm up race.

The racers all stopped, or should we say fell off their camels, they were laughing so hard. Jamshid was nearly hysterical. Wolf got up and shook himself off and gazed at the cut straps on his saddle and his eyes immediately fell on Jamshid.

"I know it was you, you little thief!" he bellowed, and took off in a run after Jamshid. He chased him around for about ten minutes all the time cursing and screaming obscenities at him until at last Jamshid was in his grasp. Jamshid put up a valiant struggle but he was no match for Wolf's iron grip and he soon found himself deposited in the waters of the oasis pond.

After drying out and waiting for the night to fall this tired group of friends watched the fire burn and realised the friendships they shared were strong but not permanent, and for now they would enjoy them.

Po had silently watched all of this drama unfolding as the months turned into years and he wasn't happy about it. Po didn't like the fact that the sultan was playing a dangerous game with his own daughter and the three young princes. He understood why the sultan was doing this, as there were few in the palace court that could be trusted.

After their rescue Jamshid and Eskandar were given their freedom and employed as agents of the sultan. Each man had qualifications suited to espionage work. Jamshid was a former thief and could scale walls and gain access to areas that other men couldn't, and Eskandar was an intelligent giant of a warrior that few men would want to argue with, his size matched his brain, and he could be trusted.

Over the course of Jamie's stay these two emissaries would visit often and after reporting to the sultan they would seek each other out for news, horseplay and drink. Most of their spy missions were routine, but this time they had heard rumours of a coup being planned, and they were receiving mixed messages from some of the hill tribes and it worried them.

Their stay would be short this time, as they had to try and find out why the hills and desert were so quiet. Someone would have had to pay out a lot of gold to keep it so. It was their job to try and find out who was paying it. This was the reason they had been summoned to return to the palace.

Wolf was always happy to see Eskandar as they were the same size and Wolf felt like he was talking to an equal when they conversed.

When Wolf and Eskandar marched through the market square it was a sight to behold as these two giant men presented a striking contrast to one another. Wolf's flowing blonde hair that was bleached nearly white by the desert sun and piercing blue eyes and flowing beard gave him a mystical appearance. Eskandar looked as though his body had been chiselled from stone and the desert sun only reflected away from a piercing set of red eyes.

Strangely very few people ever troubled them, but occasionally someone would try. While on one particular outing the two were relaxing at a local eatery they were approached by two men looking for trouble. Because of the way they were seated and wearing cloaks their antagonists couldn't tell what size men they were. They were not happy when they found out!

Standing up and removing their cloaks, Wolf and Eskandar towered above their opponents and one could see the look of sheer terror in their eyes as they realised what manner of men they had confronted. Quickly they apologised saying it was a case of mistaken identity and then swiftly made for their camels and rode away as fast as they could. They thanked Allah for sparing their lives this day.

This motley crew of assorted friends and acquaintances that surrounded the three young princes would have many more adventures before they left for home. Some of their adventures would be filled with wonderment and others would be very costly in terms of lives that would be lost or changed forever by the fates.

Time alters everyone's destiny and nobody can escape this.

PALACE LIFE

The princess came to visit the boys or more to the point, Jamie regularly every day and as she came to know these sons of kings a little more, she liked them and her servant Sarah had taken quite a liking to Liam as well.

Such wild and free men she had never met the like of before. As they trained and the days turned into weeks she learned of their customs and legends, and of their hopes and dreams. The religious and tales of the druids fascinated her the most. By all accounts she learned that these priests were very intelligent with much knowledge on a wide range of subjects. Aza also learned that they could be a very deadly sect when angered. This was something she could identify with, as fanatics were nothing new in her land.

Aza was extremely interested in the marriage customs of their land, something not uncommon for a young woman of marrying age to think about. What fascinated her most was the idea that a woman could choose her own mate. In her land all or most of the marriages were arranged or bargained for.

Many of Aza's friends had been married off to corpulent old men and were not very happy… she wanted to be happy.

The expatriate kings were also learning much of this land and each day the streams of travellers passing through the city from far off distant lands to destinations unknown assaulted their senses.

Each day they saw a new variety of people, they saw Nubians, black as ebony, yellow Chinese and Mongolians, Egyptians, Greeks and a score of other races and tribes that passed through these lands to trade or seek adventure. All were richly costumed and perfumed, resplendent in their jewels.

A parade of strange animals such as camels, caged gorillas and elephants carrying large cargoes, along with exotic cats on long leashes, and giraffes passed by them daily, before their bewildered eyes. The scents of rare perfumes and spices, along with scented flowers and the smells of strange foods and delicacies hammered at their senses.

This was like living in a magical kingdom for them; it was a world they never knew existed. The wealth of this land was incredible and the army that guarded it and kept the peace was enormous. Few from the peasant class or neighbouring kingdoms would dare try to upset its balance.

The sultan had enemies within his own palace. Various members of his governing council and advisors dreamt of the sultan's wealth and power, many wondered how they could obtain it.

The plans of these men were ruined when the princess was rescued. Had she been lost at sea, all of their problems would have been solved. The cost of hiring the pirates had drained most of their finances, as well as the costs of their new arrangement.

The schemes of these power hungry men were starting to unravel at a rapid pace. They had spent much gold and received little for their money. Part of the bribe to the pirates was to ensure that in the future their ships wouldn't be attacked. They needed a new plan.

These three new friends of the sultan would have to be worked into the scheme of things so that if anything went wrong the blame would fall to them. After all what did it matter that three infidels would die.

Azeem was a wealthy merchant whose caravans from the south and east supplied a continuous stream of spices, rare woods, slaves, jewels and other sundry merchandise throughout the land. The inner workings of the kingdom were filled with men on his payroll and many in court owed him favours. It would soon be time for him to collect on those favours.

This would-be sultan was well educated and he had been a soldier before entering the world of commerce. He quickly became a sharp and confident trader with a certain kind of charisma that would be used to get what he needed from people.

A meeting was arranged between the co-conspirators and himself, it was decided that Afghan assassins be hired. Time was running out. Agents of Azeem's would steal the swords of Jamie, Liam, and Wolf to eliminate the royal family and these would be left at the scene of the crime proving their guilt.

Justice moved swiftly in this land and they would be found guilty, executed and then the way to the throne would be open. If things went as well as they planned there would be very few questions asked, and still fewer people left to ask any questions.

A smile went across Azeem's face as he thought about what he would do as a ruler, where his word was law, and his sword feared by many nations. Power coursed through his veins just thinking about it. He would enjoy this, he smugly thought to himself. His Afghan assassins would get the job done; he had never known them to fail before.

The prince was due to arrive the next week for his marriage to Princess Aza. This would be the perfect time to put their plans into action. They could not do it when the prince came, for if anything happened to him during the takeover, it might mean war between their two countries.

Young James Cameron was not particularly thrilled about the princess's upcoming marriage either, how could he be for he was in love with her and he didn't know what to do about it. He tried to keep these thoughts out of his mind by keeping busy, but it didn't do much good. There were many preparations to make for the long journey home, and the battles they would have to win in order to claim their birth rights, the fight he had going on within himself, was as fierce as any of his future battles would be. Those he could fight with honour, but there was no honour in leaving Aza.

At last the day came, and Prince Jamshid arrived amidst the sound of trumpets and a great procession made its way to the sultan's palace. In the days previous the court and its many chambers were dusted and cleaned by an army of servants. The palace servants scurried about like ants making sure that everything was prepared in time for the royal wedding.

There was probably enough wine shipped in to fill a small lake and great mounds of food had been cooking all day. The aromas of flowers placed in large urns along with the myriad scents floating through the air created an atmosphere of mystery and intrigue in the cool night of the desert.

Rizhad was going to see to it that the nobles and guests of the sultan remained safe during their stay. He tripled the palace guard and ordered his men to question anyone who appeared suspicious. Rizhad was taking no chances.

Unfortunately Jamie and Aza didn't follow this line of thinking. That night the princess made her way to Jamie's quarters much to his surprise.

"What are you doing here?" He grabbed her arms forcibly at the same time. "Are you trying to get me killed? This is the night before your wedding, if you are found here we will both die," he exclaimed.

"Please don't be angry," she replied. "I had to see you, it is the last time I will be able to speak with you as an equal. Tomorrow it would be forbidden. I am in such turmoil I don't know what to do." He pulled her closer and into the shadows of the night so as not to be seen. As he held her tightly she felt so warm, sensuous and alive, and he wanted to take her right there but knew that he couldn't. He broke away from her and moved farther back into the shadows.

"My mind is confused and I don't know the right thing to do anymore. I love you and I cannot have you, by tomorrow I will be married to a man that I hardly know, and I'm not sure that I want to be his bride. On the other hand I know where my duties lie as a princess and what I must do but it still torments me. Oh why does love have to be so confusing?" she asked Jamie.

"I don't know, it's a mystery to me as well, for I know I never planned for any of this to happen," he replied. "Perhaps love is an intangible thing that has no answers." He took her in his arms and embraced her for a brief moment that felt like hours. Holding her for what was probably the last time he couldn't help but wonder why life was so unfair, and why things never seemed to run smoothly. Such is life.

Sneaking Aza back to her chambers, a thousand things now danced across his mind. Should he stay? Could he stay and change things? Could he give up his birthright? He realised he couldn't, and he couldn't betray the sultan who had been like a father to them. Nor could he risk bringing down the wrath of the sultan on them.

Jamie knew from what he had seen and heard that white skinned people were tolerated here, but very few remained in the region for long, those that did were mostly traders, and merchants. This is not to say they were ill treated, it was more that they weren't trusted by anyone.

Knowing that he must return home to reclaim his kingdom and take care of his family bothered him for he knew he could never return to this world he found himself thrust into. What bothered him the most apart from losing Aza was the fact that both he and his cousins were enjoying their new life here and felt quite comfortable with the people in this land.

A tired and confused James Cameron rounded the corner to his chambers and understood why Master Po had put them through the combat drills over and over again. He instinctively ducked as he heard the whistle of the scimitar's blade pass over his head. His reflexes had been sharpened to the point where his reaction had become second nature.

The arm that wielded the scimitar was that of the former captain of the guards who had sworn he would make Jamie pay for his demotion. Had he struck a couple of seconds earlier his revenge would have been complete, he wouldn't get another chance. After ducking Jamie immediately went into a roll and came up with his sword drawn. As he did two more assailants appeared from behind some curtains.

Jamie recognised them as two of the guards that had been demoted with the captain and they were strong swordsmen. He was in trouble now for most of the palace was asleep. The two guards thought these infidels curried too much of the sultan's favour, favour they thought they deserved.

Now facing three swordsman instead of one, Jamie attacked, being outnumbered he didn't have much of a choice. Lunging at the nearest swordsman he sidestepped, ducked, and ran his sword across the belly of the former captain. In one almost fluid movement, the captain's life was over. Now the others, the two remaining guards now realised they were facing a superior swordsman and decided to attack Jamie from opposite sides and at the same time always pressing the attack forward. These were strong swordsmen and Jamie ducked, parried and slashed, moving like a whirlwind between them and was beginning to get worn down. A glancing blow from one of the guards had opened a large gash on his left upper arm.

The noise had awoken Rizhad who entered the room with sword drawn. He could see Jamie was having a hard time and bleeding on his left side.

Jamie caught the movement of Rizhad's entry into the room in the corner of his eyes, and in the dim light wasn't sure if he was being attacked by another guard and turned to parry his blow. That split second allowed one of the guards to find an opening and slice a large deep cut across Jamie's right thigh causing him to collapse on the floor.

Rizhad stepped in between Jamie and his attackers and ended the conflict with lightning speed. Driving his sword through the ribcage of one guard, he turned and removed the head from the other guard. He would have been dead had it not been for Rizhad's quick thinking. One of the guards had his sword raised to finish Jamie off when Rizhad stepped in. Both of the dead guards had surprised looks on their faces, even the headless one.

The commotion had aroused the whole palace and the assorted people entering the room were shocked at the carnage. There was blood everywhere. Jamie was in trouble. Rizhad had been holding his hand over Jamie's wound and now removed his tunic to wrap around Jamie's leg to try and stop the bleeding.

Po had sent for the physicians who attended Jamie promptly and carried him away to further attend his condition.

Jamie's wounds were very serious; he had lost a lot of blood and was bleeding from two different wounds, and other assorted cuts and bruises. There was no way of knowing if he would survive this attack, only time would answer that question.

The sultan was informed of the attack and was furious; he would go to Jamie's side at once. Seeing the extent of Jamie's wounds disturbed him, he had seen these kinds of wounds many times before and few men survived them. Disturbed by what he saw he left the chambers shaking his head and cursing.

While returning to his chamber the sultan was greeted by Prince Rashid, his future son-in-law. Being quartered in a different wing of the palace, he was not aware of what had happened and was only informed by a servant a short time ago.

The prince enquired about Jamie and requested to see him. The sultan granted his request, and the physicians would be done by the time they reached his chamber. Upon entering his room, his breathing told the story, but he was alive.

"So this is the man you told me of, great sultan, indeed he has the look of a fierce warrior," Rashid said.

"Yes," replied the sultan. "If it were not for him, I would be daughterless and you would be wifeless. Our two kingdoms would then probably be immersed in some sort of turmoil as well. The courage of these three young men is remarkable, they fear very little, but his wounds are of grave concern to me."

"Do not fear great sultan, the Gods have spared him for greater things. Why already the legend of this man and his companions is spreading throughout the land. Many of my own escort volunteered for this journey in the hope of meeting your guests. He is young and strong and will survive this."

Prince Rashid spoke with great conviction, but the sultan wasn't so sure, and his affection for Jamie clouded the issue.

Thanking the prince for his concern, they both decided not to wake Jamie and each returned to his quarters to prepare for the wedding. The sultan did so with a heavy heart, there was much to worry about; a kingdom was at stake.

Rizhad was in a foul mood. He had little sleep that night and ordered the entire palace guard assembled in the courtyard where he gave then their final orders for the wedding and feast. He also delivered a final warning to them.

"Last night three members of the guard attacked a friend of mine and now he lies on death's doorstep. Let it be known that these men are personal friends of mine and any more acts of treachery against them will be considered an attack against me personally. You will not like my response. The heads of the three murderers are mounted on the gate of the guards headquarters as a reminder for you." Rizhad was mad and he went on. "If anyone violates this edict, I will have your entire families boiled alive in front of you, your property will be confiscated, and you will have much to think about as you are marched to the copper mines where you will end your days!"

The guards were upset at the treachery of last night for many had become friends with the three young princes and spent much time in their company. These guards would see to it that it was a joyful celebration.

"You have your orders," Rizhad added. "See to it that nothing like this happens again, for if it does, there will be nothing in heaven or earth that will spare you from the sultan's anger or my wrath. Now be off, and follow your orders."

Finally the day of Aza's wedding came. She was dressed in a light blue gown with gold sequins throughout in a flowing pattern. The gown trailed to the floor and combined with her jewellery she looked stunning. She had been coifed, combed and perfumed like never before. The ruby necklace she wore shone like fire against her skin, but it gave no warmth to her.

While dressing, she had many things on her mind and Jamie was right at the top of the list. She could not go to him for that would be an insult to both her father and her soon to be husband. Her thoughts were filled with Jamie's image and even during her wedding vows she couldn't get him out of her mind. Not knowing if the man she truly loved would live or die gnawed at her soul.

The ceremony was not very long and she was soon married. The prince looked very handsome in his black silk robe, it was embroidered with lacework and gold tracery throughout.

While the words were being read, she wondered if she would be able to love him with the same passion as Jamie, in any event it would probably not be unpleasant, and she had little choice in the matter now.

The feasting would go on for many days, but tonight she had to play the role of congenial host. She received her guests and well-wishers with the utmost grace as her new status required it, she was a queen now.

Later that evening as Aza entered the bridal chamber to consummate the marriage, she knew there was no turning back.

When in the prince's arms she realised he was a caring and thoughtful lover, who respected her shyness and propriety. Perhaps she could learn to love him as she had Jamie, she thought to herself. During their lovemaking her only desire was to have Jamie's strong arms around her, and these thoughts encouraged her to reach new levels of orgasmic delight she never knew existed. The prince was particularly satisfied with himself, thinking that it was he that aroused such intense pleasure in his new queen.

During their lovemaking the prince noticed some hesitancy in his wife's responses, and wasn't sure if it was shyness or some other reason that caused this. Perhaps it was some forbidden secret he did not yet know? Holding her in his arms he didn't really care, she was his wife and would provide him with heirs to two thrones. Soon both he and the princess were fast asleep for it had been a long day.

The feasting would go on for several days and things were good, for James Cameron they weren't. He tossed and turned for several days as the fever, which had come with his wounds burnt itself out. It was astonishing that he had the strength to fight off the fever as he had lost a dangerous amount or blood and was very weak. He was so weak he couldn't even raise his arm to drink with; the physicians had to do it for him.

Liam and Wolf had been away for a few days and knew nothing of his condition until their return. They weren't happy with what they saw; this could change everything.

On the second day of feasting, the prince requested to meet the other two men that saved his wife from certain death. The sultan informed him that they had just returned from a journey and would be coming to the feast. He then cursed the treachery of his own guards. Knowing that Jamie was lying on his bed fighting for his life troubled him greatly for these three had become like sons to him.

Liam and Wolf arrived a short time later and when introduced he asked them if they were Christians, they told him yes, but they still had leanings towards their own priests and beliefs. Christianity had existed in the British Isles for many years, but like all new things, people were hesitant and many clung to the old ways.

Upon looking at Wolf the prince asked, "Are all the men of your land of such stature and size as you?"

With a mischievous look from those steel blue eyes, Wolf replied, "No, great prince, I'm the smallest one of the litter, the rest of my family are much larger." Everybody laughed.

"By all that's holy, I hope I never have to feast your family, it would take most of the sheep and cattle in my small kingdom to feed them, and probably most of our crops." The prince had his joke and everyone laughed till their sides ached.

The night's feasting continued and the prince sat back enjoying the revelry around him. He enjoyed the company of Wolf and Liam and was anxious to meet Jamie. He had many questions.

The stories he had heard of Jamie made him all the more curious, as did the look in Aza's eyes whenever his name was mentioned.

The sultan informed his guests that the prince and his new queen would be extending their stay. The former princess had many things to pack, and several things that she had to attend to before she could begin her new life. This was the only excuse that he could think of. There was no point in telling his guests they were staying so the prince could meet Jamie.

Her servant Sarah, who had been spending time with Liam, kept Aza informed of Jamie's progress. The only thing she could tell Aza was that Jamie still had the fever and it was still touch and go if he would survive.

Four days later the fever broke and Jamie regained consciousness. He managed to drink some water and swallow a little broth before falling asleep again. Three days later, his condition had much improved.

Several visitors came to see Jamie even though he was still very weak. The first visitor was Rizhad and it brought a smile to Jamie's face.

"It is good to see you recovering at last James," he said.

"They tell me I wouldn't be here if it wasn't for you saving my life. I thank you. What happened?"

"The old captain of the guards swore an oath against you, he thought you were responsible for getting him demoted and talked the other two dogs into joining him. Knowing that you would be leaving soon he decided to take a chance and try and kill you because he knew he wouldn't get the opportunity when you were gone. Having you killed would look bad for the sultan, and make my leadership of the guard look bad. Do not worry my friend, they are now sitting at hell's gate, awaiting entrance, and I'm sure it will be a very long wait, as they were also ugly."

Rizhad laughed hard and even Jamie managed a small laugh himself. This hurt a lot as he was still very weak. Jamie would carry a small limp for the rest of his life because of this attack. His right arm would heal, but his broken heart wouldn't.

Growing weary Jamie's weakened voice ordered Rizhad out. "Get out of here and let me rest, if you stay any longer I'll just break open my wounds laughing at your nonsense."

"Very well," Rizhad said. "I will return later tomorrow afternoon to visit you, for now I have to attend to my duties of the palace and many other important matters that an infidel like you wouldn't understand. I don't get to lounge around, and be waited on hand and foot like some people I know."

"Get out!" Jamie said with a smile on his face, and with that reached over and grabbed a persimmon from the bowl of fruit, placed next to his bed and using his good arm made a feeble attempt to throw it at Rizhad's head, missing entirely.

Rizhad's laughter echoed down the hallway as he left Jamie's chamber.

Smiling, Jamie was soon fast asleep, Wolf and Liam dropped by, but seeing the condition he was in, decided not to wake him.

The sultan came for a visit next but couldn't stay long for his daughter would be leaving soon to begin her new life. There was also the business of the court to minister to.

Jamie slept until the early evening and when he awoke it was to the sight of Aza sitting on the edge of his bed.

"How are you?" he asked her. The former princess leaned over and kissed him on the forehead and then after releasing him said with great tenderness, "I have been worried day and night about you, this is how I am. You were very near death's door and I feared I would never see you again. I am now married to one man and in love with another and have never been so confused in my life."

Jamie did his best to reassure her that their love could never be and it was hopeless to think otherwise. Unfortunately this didn't help very much, but he didn't know what else to say.

They sat in awkward silence for a long while and Aza held him for the last time and then returned to the feast that she cared little about.

Wolf and Liam came by shortly after the new queen left, and drunk as they were from the feast with thoughts of returning home running through their heads, each was amazed that Jamie was still alive.

Liam spoke first. "Aye, laddie, you scared the hell out of us, even the physicians said that by all accounts you should be dead. Everyone in the palace was concerned about you."

Wolf then piped up and said, "Just so you know, cousin, we are very glad that you're not dead, we would have had to change all of our plans otherwise." They all laughed and embraced.

Jamie asked if they still wanted to go ahead with their plans, many things had already been set in motion and they told him they were leaving in a few days' time. Jamie himself would not be able to travel for at least ten to twelve weeks. The thought of them going into battle without him bothered him but there wasn't much he could do about it at the moment.

At least Wolf and Liam would gain some experience under battle conditions, he thought to himself and he would meet them in Gaul when they were ready to put phase two of their battle plan into action.

Jamie knew they were both a little hesitant because the journey home to reclaim their kingdoms was near and they didn't know what to expect or what they would find on their return.

The night before Wolf and Liam and Jamie were to say goodbye and take the step to the long journey home they were summoned to Master Po's quarters. Jamie was barely able to hobble around such were his wounds so he was carried on a dais to Po's quarters.

Po clapped his hands and three large servants dragged in three large trunks, and the three young princes were told to sit down.

Jamie was curious. He couldn't go with Liam and Wolf because of the extent of his wounds so this was all a mystery to him.

"I have a few going away gifts for you, and I think you can make use of them soon," Po stated. Opening the first metal trunk he pulled out a large metal breastplate embossed with gold plated eagles front and back on a black enamelled background. The next item was a magnificently carved helmet topped with a golden eagle's wings spread. The last item in the trunk was a silver inlaid battle-axe in the same pattern as that used by the Northmen. These he presented to Wolf. "Use these in your coming battles and remember that in combat your own great strength can be turned against you in an instant and you will lose," Po told him. "Just so you know it took most of the steel in Damascus to make these for you my large pupil."

They all broke out into laughter and for the first time they heard Po laugh. He usually just flashed that sardonic grin of his and grunted. Tonight he laughed to hide the pain of never seeing these three again. To him they had replaced the sons he lost and they were three of the best swordsmen he had ever trained. He was also very proud of them.

Moving over to Liam's trunk, Po lifted out two identical swords intricately carved in Keltic patterns with two large green emeralds embedded in the pommel. He was given these because of his mastery of the two sword techniques. Liam's breastplate was ornamented with gold crossed swords on a black enamelled background, and lastly his helmet was adorned with a gold dragon. A creature Liam knew nothing about until meeting Po. The mythology fascinated him.

"My final words to you, Liam, are if you can ever learn to control that burning temper of yours, no man will ever be able to take these swords away from you."

For his favourite pupil, James, a breastplate with three black ravens on the front of an enamelled gilt background of gold and silver tracery. The sword he received contained a flat ruby the size of a robin's egg embedded in the pommel handle, and was engraved with Keltic symbols from tip to hilt. His helmet portrayed a phoenix rising, symbolising their rise from ashes to their return to power.

"My advice to you, James, is that you must look for the good in men and learn to rule wisely and fairly. One thing that you must all learn is to hand out mercy with as much vigour as you hand out vengeance. If you don't, the anger contained within your hearts will destroy everything you have worked for."

The three soon to be kings were stunned; they had never expected any of this. The workmanship of their armour and weapons was superb and it must have cost Master Po a great deal.

All in the room were choked up, and tears welled up inside them. They hugged and backslapped for a while and then returned to their chambers for a fitful night's sleep. Tomorrow a new day would bring the promise of freedom and more adventures.

They would all miss Master Po. He had become a friend as well as a teacher, and they would miss his wise counsel.

THE CONSPIRATORS

Azeem left his concubines' quarters in the early morning and made his way through the already crowded streets of the bazaar to the palace courtyard. He was feeling very refreshed after a fine night of debauchery. Seeing Kourosh his friend he called out to him. "How are things with you, my friend?"

"They are fine," Kourosh replied.

"We need to talk, let us find a bench far away from prying eyes and ears."

Kourosh was a rich silk merchant who had been trading with the east for many years and was not happy with the news that the princess was to marry. If this marriage took place he could lose his trade concessions. This he was not prepared to do. The sultan and the princess would have to go.

"This thing must be done quickly and with no mistakes or we will all hang, or worse," Kourosh said.

"Tell me more, have the rest of our plans been put into place? Are we ready? I grow more nervous with each passing day. I fear someone will betray us," Azeem responded.

Kourosh then went on to explain that Darius, another of their co-conspirators had hired a group of assassins from the mountains of Afghanistan to do the job. He then explained to him that they were a fierce lot that smoked hashish and worked themselves into a killing frenzy. They would do the job.

"What price do these assassins seek for their services?" Azeem asked.

"They seek twenty bags of gold and some concessions on our northern trade routes after we take over."

"That is a very high price, a very high price indeed. My only concern is can they do it? And can they do it before the princess's new husband arrives?"

Kourosh continued. "I am sure they can do it, and there is no better time for us. They have been slipping men into this area for the last few days and will be ready to strike soon. They need only our final approval and it will begin."

"Very well," Azeem said. "Tell them to proceed and make sure that the others know we have started this adventure, we are running out of time for this to be successful. One more thing before you go, Kourosh, has any provision been made for the king's new friends? They seem to have a tendency to interfere in our business."

"Don't worry, Azeem, when I bargained for this, their demise is included as part of the deal, made them very happy. The Afghans said since they were infidels, they would kill them for free," Kourosh said laughingly.

Jamie and Rizhad were standing on the ramparts of the eastern wall of the palace watching the comings and goings of the market place after a hard training session from Po.

Jamie began to think about the time when he and Rizhad weren't such good friends. Rizhad was the son of a court noble that didn't want the rich life of the court; he craved more adventure so he joined the palace guard. When Master Po began training Jamie and the others, he began to resent them, until their arrival he was Master Po's top pupil and now Po gave all his extra attention to these infidels. Things were bound to get heated and during one training session a sword duel broke out between Jamie and Rizhad that could have ended up with someone killed if Master Po hadn't intervened.

Once Po had separated and calmed both combatants down, he called both boys onto the mats. Shaking his head back and forth, walking in front of them, Po suddenly wheeled around and snap kicked Rizhad, knocking him unconscious, before his feet landed, he delivered an elbow smash to Jamie that sent him to dreamland. When they awoke and collected their wits, Po had all the students sit in the lotus position while he lectured them on why they were there.

"This is not a contest!" he yelled. "It is a training hall for you to learn the arts of war. Some of you will be carrying many responsibilities when you leave here. One thing you had better learn to control is your anger before it clouds your vision when in combat."

Po continued. "Many men have come at me with a sharp sword and with anger in their eyes, they have all been buried. Rizhad, you are one of my better students and you should know better than to engage in stupid brawls. As for you Jamie, you have a quick temper and you must learn to control it or it will get the better of you. Since you two enjoy each other's company so much, I have decided that you should spend more time together. For the next two weeks, you two are assigned to cleaning out the horse and camel stables of the palace. Now get out of my sight!"

Master Po dismissed the class so he could keep a watchful eye on them, as he figured they would be fighting again within the hour, at least they wouldn't be fighting here, also a couple of weeks of shovelling manure night smarten them up.

He was wrong of course; it took only twenty minutes before they were going at it again. Things escalated when Rizhad sent a shovel load of manure flying that hit Jamie in the back of the head. Jamie responded by firing a shovel load of manure at Rizhad point blank in the face and then they started to trade punches and kicks. Jamie hit Rizhad with a one-two combination that knocked him down while Rizhad retaliated with a leg sweep that sent him sprawling into a fresh pile of manure. They traded blows for the next fifteen minutes, but neither would give in.

A short time later they both collapsed on a pile of straw, bloody and battered and covered in manure. Realising it was useless to go on as they were too evenly matched, they called it a draw and returned to the palace. Most of the servants kept a respectable distance from them. While at the same time, quickly prepared baths for them.

"I don't know, but I think the servants think you smell bad, James Cameron," Rizhad said.

"Is that right?" Jamie responded. "I thought covered in blood and shit as you are, they were probably scared that you might be a demon incarnate."

Both young men were scrubbed down, wounds patched, and fed like they hadn't eaten in a week. After this these tired young men went to bed and slept like the dead.

The next day on the way to the stables, Rizhad remarked to Jamie, "You know infidel, I have fought many men in my short lifetime and few have been able to go the distance with me. In time I could even tolerate your company," he said with a smile.

Smiling back at him Jamie replied, "Well if the palace guard can tolerate that ugly face of yours, I guess I could get used to it as well." They both laughed and Jamie held out his hand. Rizhad took Jamie's hand and from that day on they were the best of friends. Acting like they were brothers at times. Sharing many adventures.

Once Jamie's thoughts had returned to the present, he asked Rizhad. "Who are those fierce looking men I see down there? They are all riding black horses and I've never seen that manner of dress before."

"They look like Afghans, Jamie, but I'm not sure they don't usually travel this far west. They usually stay in their mountains. They are a fierce tribe of men. Let's go have a closer look at these mountain warriors."

With that the two ran down the balcony and into the street like a couple of kids chasing a cat. Once they got nearer and saw the brands on their horses and smelled the pungent sweet smell of hashish, Rizhad was certain they were Afghans.

"They don't look any tougher than anyone else I've seen in this part of the world," Jamie exclaimed.

"Maybe not," Rizhad replied. "I'm not getting a good feeling about this. I think we should tell Master Po. If these are not the kind of men to fool with, they trade in opiates, sell slaves, smoke hashish and they are absolutely fearless." Rizhad was getting a bad feeling about this. He turned and grinning said to Jamie, "With your poor swordsmanship, I fear for you. We must go."

Smiling back Jamie replied, "Well since you live in fear, we had better get Master Po to hold your hand, child. After you my delicate flower."

Master Po had just finished a short training session with a new group of students and was annoyed when the two burst back into his class.

"What are you two dung warriors doing back in my class? Your training session is over for today. Go back to the barn and get back to work!" *Laughter from the class.*

"We're sorry, Master, but we have seen something that you should take a look at. It concerns the safety of the palace."

Once they were outside, the boys explained to him what they had seen. He wanted a closer look, so he and Jamie slowly filtered into the market place. After taking a good long look, Po told Rizhad to double the palace guard on his authority and sent Jamie to find Liam and Wolf.

"I think you boys are right, I don't like the look of these strangers. Their eyes tell me that they are not merchants, but cold-blooded killers. Meet me back at the training hall after sundown and bring your swords.

Just after sundown, the boys returned to the hall and told Master Po what they had learned from talking with the merchants. The strangers asked a lot of unusual questions; like how many troops were garrisoned at the palace; where the guards were quartered; and questions about the palace in general. Not the usual questions that a merchant would normally ask. Master Po was getting worried, something just didn't feel right.

Po told the boys that for some time now the sultan had been aware that several members of his court were involved in a conspiracy to upset his rule, and he was aware that some of the conspirators were among his closest advisors and friends. Several members of the court were not happy with the upcoming marriage of the princess. Many felt that the loss of their trade concessions would only give the sultan more power.

This was sheer nonsense for as a ruler in this part of the world, the sultan was a firm but fair sovereign. His people did not suffer under his reign, and their burdens were light. Such is the foolishness of men, Po thought to himself.

"Perhaps we should take turns guarding the sultan and the princess tonight. I feel an evil presence here tonight and I cannot shake the feeling," Po stated. "Jamie, you and Wolf go to the princess's chamber, the guards will hardly notice your presence as you spend so much time there," he said with a twinkle in his eye.

A red-faced Jamie grabbed Wolf and headed towards her chamber, he could not help the fact that he had fallen in love with her, when it comes to affairs of the heart rationality cannot force the mind to accept things as they are, the sultan and most of the court knew they were in love with each other, but they all knew she was promised to another man, and so did Jamie, but how could he walk away? Po had ordered Liam and Rizhad to the sultan's chambers and left to check on the guards.

It was around eleven o'clock in the evening by the time Po had made it to the guards' chamber. Noticing that the guard had fallen asleep, he went over to reprimand him and realised that this guard would never wake up. A pool of blood told him the story. Immediately Po unsheathed his sword and went into a cat stance, creeping slowly down the corridor to the guards' quarters he came upon a grisly scene.

Twenty of the palace guard had been murdered in their sleep; their throats had been cut while they were dreaming. They would dream no more. Experts, skilled in the art of stealth, carried out this bloody attack. He knew this to be true for he had trained most of these guards and they were not easy men to sneak up on.

His senses barely recovered from the carnage he had just witnessed. Po moved further into the guards' chamber and instinctively ducked as a sword whistled past his head out of the darkness. His attacker made only one mistake, he missed Po. That cost him his life as Po quickly drove the point of his sword through the attacker's heart.

Just as he was recovering from this attack, three more would be assassins came at him out of the darkness. Picking up another sword from the floor, Po came at them with a flurry of two sword techniques and attacks the like of which few had ever seen. Po knew the only way to beat this many foes was to attack. Two of them quickly went down. The third man wasn't so easy to take down, he was a skilled swordsman and refused to yield. After what seemed like five minutes Po's sword finally found his mark and the third attacker went to meet his god.

A sweating and tired Po ran over to the palace gong and struck it many times. Any further attacks would be without surprise as the gong could be heard through the whole palace arousing everyone.

Liam and Rizhad were almost at the sultan's chambers when they heard the gong ringing. They made their way over several bodies strewn about the hallway, both guards and attackers.

The sultan was an excellent swordsman and warrior as he proved that night. Upon entering the sultan's chamber they witnessed the sultan removing the head from his attacker's body. There were several other bodies scattered throughout the sultan's chamber. He had been very busy.

Seeing the boys, the sultan quickly asked them, "Is the princess all right and safe?"

Rizhad assured him that she was safe as Wolf and Jamie had gone to her aid.

"We are going there right now, if you are all right, and with your permission."

"Go, and don't worry about me," the sultan told them. How the sultan wished he had sons like these four. With men like them at my side, he mused to himself, I could conquer the world.

Jamie, upon entering the princess's chamber, noticed her maidservant lying on the floor unconscious but still alive. Before he could call out, a movement from the corner of his eye caused him to duck and roll bringing his sword upwards in a twisting motion. His sword pierced the attacker's vital organs and he fell in a heap to the floor. Master Po's training had paid off.

Out of the darkness four more men attacked and Jamie fought for his life, thrust, parry, block, attack, feint. It was a ferocious battle and Jamie was clearly outnumbered.

Suddenly one of his attackers seemed to fly through the air, screaming his last breath as he was launched over the balcony to the courtyard below. Jamie smiled, for he knew without looking that it was the powerful arms of his cousin Wolf that sent his attacker over the balcony.

Liam then appeared through another exit and took out one of the swordsmen attacking Jamie; this allowed Jamie to put his attacker down. The fourth assassin tried to make it out the door but found himself pinned to it as Rizhad's sword flew through the air in a spinning arc impaling him to it.

Liam asked if the princess was safe.

At that moment she came out of where she was hidden and ran into Jamie's arms. She was safe at last. If anyone in the palace was unaware of how these two felt about each other that mystery was solved tonight.

The whole palace was awake by now and it would be nearly daylight before anyone would get to sleep with all the commotion and bodies lying everywhere. A contingent of what was left of the palace guard were lining up the dead Afghans in rows to be buried.

"What are Afghans doing here?" the sultan asked. "Someone must have paid a lot of gold to send this man," he stated.

Shortly after this, the captain, his guards and the boys were summoned to the sultan's chamber.

The sultan was furious, an attack on the battlefield was one thing, but to have his family attacked in his own home in his presence would not be tolerated. The captain of his guard was the first to feel the sultan's wrath.

"Tell me, Captain Ezra, what is it I pay you and your guards to do, sit around and sleep and get fat? Where were my loyal guards when I needed them most? These are dangerous times and you lighten the guard around my palace! Have you gone insane? If it wasn't for the sharp eyes and intervention of my guests, my family would be lying about me!"

The sultan stared at him for a long time and then said, "You have been a faithful and loyal captain of my guard so I will not lop off your head this time. I will, however, be giving your post to another. You may return to the ranks as sergeant. I'll issue orders later regarding you."

The captain, humiliated, left quickly for if the sultan ever found out that it was he who shortened the list of guards on duty so the Afghans would have an easier time getting to the key areas of the palace, he would surely lose his head. He now had three more names to add to his list of enemies: Jamie, Liam and Wolf. He didn't care about Rizhad, because he was part of the guard. He had never liked these infidels anyway and only tolerated them because of the sultan. He vowed to pay them back for this

After the guard left, the sultan had a muffled conversation with Master Po, and then turned towards Rizhad and asked him, "What position do you hold in the guard, and what is your rank?"

"I am a Sergeant at Arms, first rank," Rizhad replied.

"Not anymore, from now on, you are the Head Captain of the Palace Guard and Master of Arms for the palace. Po tells me that your mind is as sharp as your sword and that you are loyal. See that you stay that way for I need loyal men in my guard. I will not forget what you did here tonight."

The sultan dismissed them and returned to his chambers to sleep, it had been a long night.

Outside the sultan's chambers the boys congratulated Rizhad on his new command, and then began teasing him.

Wolf was the first to speak up. "Well my friends, I guess we will have to bow and salute when 'Captain' Rizhad walks by us."

"Well of course," Liam replied, "but after we salute will he want us to bring him young maidens dipped in honey next?"

"Quiet!" the new Captain of the Guards spoke. "Do not provoke me or I will have your eyeball smeared with this same honey and watch as the ants devour your eyes slowly. I will let you off this time as I am in a good mood, and I have many duties to attend to and would not have the time to fully enjoy it anyway, now be off!"

After a few more minutes of laughing and horsing around, Rizhad did have to excuse himself to attend to his new duties.

"Where's Jamie?" Liam asked Wolf.

"He was here a minute ago, but my guess is that we can find him in the princess's chambers," he said with a smile.

Sure enough five minutes later, as they entered Aza's chamber, they found the two locked in passionate embrace.

Whispering Liam said to Wolf, "Are you seeing what I'm seeing? We have to speak to him about this again."

"Yar," Wolf replied. "I don't like what I'm seeing, if he's not careful, we might end up staked out on that ant hill after all."

As they silently walked towards the happy couple, two cloaked assassins came from behind one of the hanging tapestries, swords drawn ready to cut down Aza and Jamie. Wolf charged the man nearest to him, and after knocking him to the floor, pulled out his war axe and dispatched the assassin. These murdering dogs really earn their money, Wolf thought to himself. They are persistent.

Liam was having a little trouble with his opponent, as he was an excellent swordsman, but Liam neatly dispatched the cutthroat by lopping his head off after a feint followed by a straight-handed horizontal strike. The severed head rolled about three feet away from a stunned Jamie. Everything had happened so fast.

The noise and commotion saw Rizhad come through the door leading three of his guards. Sheathing their swords, Rizhad glanced, around the room and knew immediately what had happened. He was just glad that no one got hurt. He ordered an immediate search, room by room, of the entire palace, including the sultan's chambers.

After he left the room, Liam and Wolf pulled Jamie aside and to the end of Aza's chamber and gave him hell.

"Are you trying to get us all killed?" Liam asked.

"What do you mean?" Jamie responded.

"Well for a start, Jamie, you damn near got killed a few minutes ago, and secondly you know the princess is promised to another man. This means you can't have her, what part of that don't you understand?"

Wolf spoke up next. "You know these people don't take kindly to people messing with their women. Keep this up and we will all lose our heads, think about it."

Jamie was angry, but after a few moments of thought, he realised they were right. She did belong to another man. Love does strange things to a man, he mused. How can I walk away? Why do I have to?

After this long night they all went to bed for a long sleep and some minor medical treatment. In the following days, Jamie avoided Aza as much as he could and spent more time training,

Master Po noticed the difference in him right away. Po had difficulty in holding his own in against Jamie during a single combat match with him. Had the match gone on much longer, Po would have lost.

A few days after his match with Jamie, Po called the boys into his chamber for tea.

"I called you boys or men I should say, to discuss a few things with you. There isn't much more that I can teach you for you have all become excellent swordsmen, among the finest I have ever trained. The other day I nearly lost a match to Jamie. Liam can nearly match me, and Wolf's sheer size and strength would overpower me."

Continuing on he said, "I have also noticed a growing restlessness with the three of you. Perhaps you need to start thinking about your return home. You must fulfil your destiny."

Talking amongst themselves while drinking tea, a drink they had never heard of before coming here, it was decided that Master Po was right. They had begun their journey six years ago and it was time to go and restore their families and titles, if any were left.

These three young princes had no idea of what they would be facing on their return. Leaving as boys and returning as conquering warriors would be something to go down in history and perhaps inspire other men.

Jamie decided that they should seek an audience with the sultan, not that it was needed for they often stopped at the sultan's chambers to talk or play chess.

In some ways the sultan who had no living sons of his own, came to consider them as his sons. Even though they were tutored and guided about the culture of this land, they still retained a certain wildness he couldn't explain.

It would be a bitter departure for all as new bonds of friendship had formed in this strange land and it would be tough to leave them behind.

Master Po listened to their conversation and was downhearted as well for along with Rizhad he had never trained better swordsmen in his life. He knew they would become legends in their own lands, as they had become legends here.

Po stepped out onto the balcony of his room and gazed at the stars while pondering the twists and turns of life.

THE MAD KING

King William quickly solidified his new kingdom by stamping out any opposition to his rule, and going so far as to annex some of the smaller kingdoms surrounding his. William was generous to be sure and he divided up the spoils of vanquished clans evenly among his allies. The choicest spoils he kept for himself. He was becoming a rich king, and spread his wealth to ensure the loyalty of his co-conspirators.

With each conquest he turned this land into a land of misery and suffering. Outright slavery had not existed in this country before William's conquests and the larger kingdoms he hadn't attacked were appalled at the stories that were told about William's rule. Things were no better in Ireland; the main gold producing mine required a steady stream of workers and slaves, happily supplied by William and his allies.

The Druid priest that helped Fiona end her life had been disposed of, but now William embarked on a reign of terror against any Druids he could find. Many fled to distant lands.

Those priests that survived William's wrath swore a terrible oath against him. In future they would provide services to Jamie, and his cousins, for now they would bide their time.

The first year of the new king's reign brought about many changes. The castle was expanded and enlarged moats were deepened and re-dug, and new fields were planted. Trade had been increased with his allies and this proved lucrative as well.

William's conquests and alliances gave him virtual control of a large part of northern Scotland and he was very pleased with himself. The dead queen's daughter was twelve at the time of her capture. She was well cared for and taught all the things that young ladies were supposed to know.

Brigid Cameron was a fiery redhead in both colour and temperament and resented being held captive in her own home. She had over the years developed into a beautiful woman like her mother. She was well treated in the castle and even allowed to go riding provided an escort went with her.

A gilded cage is still a cage and she longed to run and fish in the streams she once did with Jamie. Knowing that her brother and cousins were still alive kept her going and she prayed nightly for their return. Their bodies were never found and she hoped they would return to rescue her and avenge the deaths of her and Jamie's parents. It was her only hope.

King William had told no one of his plans for Brigid and had Brigid known what her uncle was planning she probably would have chosen the same path as her mother. He never bothered her and was planning to use her like an ace up his sleeve, when the time was right.

As long as William's gold flowed from the stolen mines he could be assured of the loyalty of the men he had bought. He also knew this would not last forever and used much of his gold to buy up estates in other countries that he could draw rent from in the future.

It often weighed on William's mind that his allies were cheaply bought. He provided them with gold, but where did their loyalties lie? Would they sell him out to the highest bidder or worse? Just try to assassinate him? William needed time to rebuild his army over the years and his Norse allies allowed him to accomplish this. When the time was right he would eliminate them himself.

While rebuilding his kingdom this was William's only major blunder, he had come to trust some of his Norse advisors. This was a weak link in his master plan and he would pay for it. The Norsemen were becoming rich and increasingly belligerent and stopped raiding in some areas and were expanding to more outlying posts, and had even established small posts in Russia.

Newer and larger ships were being built in the Norse shipyards, and with their holdings in Greenland and Iceland they were becoming a force to reckon with. Many of the Norse that were not allied with William were becoming envious and this envy boiled over on several occasions, Soon clashes and feuds erupted between the various factions, and they began to raid each other's shipping.

More than one land-based outpost had been attacked, and William's lunacy showed them how the power of gold could corrupt and now they were falling victim to it themselves. During William the 'mad's' reign as he was becoming known, crops were plentiful, game was aplenty, trade was lively, and yet the people of the land suffered. This would not be tolerated for long.

Many of the common folk of the land had been forced to work on the rebuilding of William's castle and had been taken from their homes and forced to work for long extended periods. Some were forced to work in the fields for starvation wages.

Older men loyal to Jamie's father remembered a time when the kings would join in their labours, whether it was building a new bridge, or bringing in the harvest. These kings worked as hard as anyone, and by joining in their labours felt their aches and pains, and sweat. This kept them a little more humble.

The older men of the village remembered all this, but for now all they could do was wait and hope that a leader might rise up to help them and lead them to freedom again. This was a forlorn hope at the moment. The castle had been rebuilt to nearly five times its original size and could now billet nearly a thousand troops with horse and armour. The storerooms contained enough supplies to withstand a very long siege.

The serfs and workmen that were forced to rebuild the castle thought they would be going home upon completion.

William decided to send them to help refortify his allies' castles once more. They would endure the lash and yoke. The workmen that installed William's new secret passages were put to the sword, the secret being William's alone.

Rebellion might be in the wind, but tonight there was revelry at the king's table, for this was the night of his annual barons meeting where his henchmen reported on their districts. By all accounts thing were going well.

The first reports from William's barons told him nothing new, some of his building projects would soon be completed, the treasury was filling nicely and everything seemed to be in order. With a drunken yawl the king started laughing and motioned for the young serving girl to sit near him. He eyed her hungrily and wondered why he had never noticed her before. She would share his bed tonight he decided.

Calling out amongst the roar of the meeting William asked, "Have there been any more complaints from my loyal subjects this eve?" William asked in a jesting, slobbering, sarcastic tone.

"All complaints so far, my lord, have been yoked and lashed," a warrior from the back of the hall yelled out.

After the laughter subsided William excused himself, and said he would return to the feast later. Grabbing the serving wench by the arm, he made a staggered effort to retire to his chamber.

The feasting would go on all night and as his hands roamed over the soft curves of her body, his thoughts returned to Fiona.

For many minutes he fumbled and cursed at his inability to perform again. In a blind rage he screamed at the girl to get dressed and get out.

The frightened girl grabbed her clothing and left as fast as she could, bewildered by William's behaviour.

Cursing Fiona's name and ranting, he fired his goblet of wine at the wall staining a large portion of it red, babbling to himself as he tried to make his way back to the feast.

Wandering to his throne, he ordered wine and mead, refilling his glass many times, finally passing out a few hours later.

Olaf had spent over a year and a half searching for Wolf with little to show for his effort. Many of the stories and leads he followed were false, and he never believed William's story that Norse Irish outlaws were the ones that attacked the castle. In several meetings with William the conversation grew heated and Olaf was tempted to run him through with his sword but refrained. His son's and nephews bodies were never found, and although he distrusted the Norse, he distrusted William even more.

Ingrid believed that her son was still alive, but for her, it was more of an intuition, a sense, a maternal bond, call it what you will. Her grief wouldn't allow her to think otherwise. She missed her son and could only hope he was well. The grief and pain she felt over this would cause future health problems.

Most women understood that some of their children would be lost to sickness, accidents, warfare, or any number of causes. To have a child vanish, not knowing if they were dead or alive was a fate worse than death. Grief weighed heavily on her for the loss of Liam and Jamie as well. She missed them all!

Only a week ago while daydreaming she remembered a time not very long ago when Wolf challenged his father to a wrestling match. After a long battle outside their lodge Olaf emerged victorious after nearly losing the match. He was glowing with pride, however, that his Fourteen-year-old son had almost bested him. Olaf did inform her that he wasn't looking forward to a return match anytime soon, and they both laughed. Ingrid knew in her heart that Olaf loved Wolf dearly and she felt the torment of not knowing as he did.

Ingrid knew that this torment he felt was worse than any battle wound he had ever suffered. Because of this she let him search on, but after nearly five years of searching she began to wonder if his search would be in vain.

Hope is a strong motivator and while on a raiding expedition that was farther south than their usual voyages Olaf learned that his son might still be alive. One of the merchants they were trading with told them that around the campfires of the desert tribes stories were being told of a giant white haired warrior and of his two red haired companions!

It is said that these men are guests of the sultan of Persia and that they are fierce and noble warriors from the cold lands to the north. The merchant could tell him little else. Promising to return in the spring, Olaf left the merchant some gold and told him that he would return with more gold in the spring, as he would be mounting an expedition to find his son.

Olaf and crew set sail for home and he wondered if this was another false lead, this was too good to be true. What were the three cousins doing in Persia? And how did they get there?

He was pleased and a smile began to appear on his haggard, worn face. Being away for the last few months he desperately wanted to share this good news with Ingrid. The trading and raiding mission had proved lucrative and each man would be returning home with a large share of gold and jewels. They traded furs, ivory, and silk for gold and jewels. These items took less room to store and were more easily divided.

Olaf's small kingdom was not as rich and powerful as those who had befriended William but it was an important one and he was still a force to be reckoned with. He was a skilled although aging warrior, a navigator, and trader. His fortune did not match some of William's allies, but he still controlled several iron and coalmines and numerous key ports.

William's gold could not buy everyone and the king of the Scots had mostly Norse and minor kings from Denmark for allies and they would not follow William's banner for long. There was already much talk about William's madness. Nothing was ever said in open court for William had spies everywhere and retaliation was swift and sudden. The men William employed did not care where the gold that filled their pouches came from, and cared less about what they had to do to earn this gold.

The one thing that Olaf did know was that William could manipulate and use people with unerring skill. He vowed he would not fall victim to William's tactics.

A week later Olaf was navigating the waters near his village and a shiver ran down his spine as he rounded the corner of the rock outcropping that said he was home. The village was very quiet and there were torches burning in front of his lodge. His heart began to beat like a drum, something was wrong, someone had died. He prayed it wasn't Ingrid. His prayers went unanswered.

Leaping from the dock before the. Longboat had even tied up, he raced to his lodge only to be met by a servant who told him of Ingrid's passing. She had died about three weeks ago from some sort of fever.

The servants had placed Ingrid's body on ice, in a small cave not far from the village to await Olaf's return. Stunned for a moment, his grief overwhelmed him and he clambered for a bench to sit on. His Ingrid was gone and just when he had news of Wolf. It wasn't fair. On the voyage home he kept thinking of how he wanted to see the look of joy on her face when he revealed his news to her, and now that chance was gone forever!

Olaf ordered Ingrid's body brought to the pier and made preparations for her funeral. This would be a small but proper Viking funeral. She was placed in a small, decorated sailboat that was set afire and then launched out to sea. Watching from the shore as the pitch blazed and crackled while it burned, he remembered the deaths of his other two children and how it had affected her.

Olaf remembered the pain both he and she felt when the village healer informed her that after Wolf she would be able to bear no more children. Ingrid bore the news with grace and dignity, maybe that was why she loved Wolf so much. He was her last child. He was very proud of her and as he watched the flames devour the boat and send his beloved to a watery grave, his hatred of William reached new depths.

Watching the last of the flames take her a maidservant spoke up and said, "She wanted you to keep looking for Wolf and to never give up, and she said she would be waiting for you in heaven or Valhalla, she didn't care where the gods would send her as long as she could be with you. I was sworn to tell you."

Olaf wasn't a poor man and now he would mount his expedition to find Wolf. Tomorrow he would send men that he could trust to scout out William and find information on Wolf. He would deal with William in his own way, in his own time.

In Norway the forges of William's allies were going strong as the demand for armour, chain mail, and weapons increased as William's army expanded. The shipyards were very busy as well building larger vessels that could be manned by larger crews and carry more cargo.

The Norse people were not forced to work like slaves but the slaves that they owned were. This was contrary to the way the Norse treated their slaves, most were not abused. Their owners however didn't have any problem spending William's gold.

The grumblings throughout the various kingdoms had been growing louder and at the castle of one of William's friends a heated discussion was taking place. Sigfried and several Norse and Danish jarls were becoming a little worried; perhaps things were going a little too smoothly. William's madness had progressed to the point where he was issuing contradictory orders and babbling to himself.

"I don't like it," Sigfried spoke up. "I know the weapons makers are getting rich supplying that mad bastard, but I don't think we should be arming these people."

"I agree," Bjorn said, "we used to raid these people at will and now we supply them with weapons. If the Scots and Irish ever learn how to use them we may never be able to raid them again."

"Don't worry," another interjected. "The one thing you can be certain of is that the Scots and Irish spend more time fighting amongst themselves than anything else. Alliances will break open and clan feuds will erupt, of this you can be sure."

"I disagree," Sigfried said loudly. "This William is smart, and ruthless, and half mad. That makes him a very dangerous man. Think about what he's accomplished in a little over five years; a good portion of Northern Scotland and a large chunk of Northern Ireland are under his control. He has also taken a ragtag group of clans and outlaws and turned them into an efficient fighting force trained in unconventional tactics."

"The Ard Ri, or high king of Ireland is planning on visiting William soon, such is his influence spreading," Gunnar said. "If this man decides to ally himself with William we could be in real trouble, and our raids would be confined to a few outlying areas."

"Enough!" Eric shouted. "The Scots and Irish are a pack of snarling dogs that bark loudly but do nothing. We could annihilate them any time we wanted. They would never attack in full force I am certain. Their speciality is hit and run tactics."

"You could be right," Sigfried replied. "Just remember that new ideas and battle tactics are harder to fight sometimes than a group of seasoned, battle hardened warriors. This madman bears watching I say, and we had better be on guard against his treachery."

After a general agreement on this and several other minor items they adjourned to quaff down many more horns of ale, and to seek out some female companionship.

During the years of William's rise to power his kingdom had been expanded but not without cost. His skill with a sword and mad treachery had united a kingdom but divided a people. The barons and ministers loyal to William lived well while the peasants or the land suffered greatly.

In the sixth year of William's reign things were going to change as the grumblings changed to anger and rebellion was near. Perhaps this was due to William's ministers now getting fat and lazy, and rich. They took few risks anymore. William's mines were played out by now and he had started to hoard his gold rather than share, this made his friends very unhappy.

Meeting with his barons and friends on a cold winter's eve, Sean O'Reagan, the man that had murdered Liam's father tried to tell the men assembled that they were squeezing too hard, and this was causing small uprisings throughout the kingdoms of both their countries.

O'Reagan never called William his king, sire, majesty or anything else; he used his given name freely. William didn't like it much but there wasn't a whole lot he could do about it either. Sean then told him of the rumours he had heard of an elite army invading England soon.

Liam and Wolf had spread these rumours on their previous visits, their trusted men saw to it that the rumours stayed in circulation. William had heard these rumours himself and dismissed them. After all why should he care if someone invades England, he had no claim there yet.

Staring at O'Reagan, William thought to himself that Sean might know something that he wasn't telling him. Tiring of his interference William decided that it was time to get rid of O'Reagan. This would be a costly mistake.

It took some time for the hall to quiet down after Sean's outburst and now it was William's turn to speak.

"If treachery and rebellion are in the wind then I suggest that you hunt down the leaders and supporters and hang or remove their heads. The rest will quickly fold. I have been wondering lately if the people in my court have grown fat and lazy with the gold and silver I have provided." Smiling at O'Reagan as he spoke, William added, "If you can't control the people in your own land that is your problem. I do have men at my disposal that could do the job for you, if you wish to hire them, Sean."

O'Reagan did not reply at first and many in the court saw the anger in his eyes and the red flush that came to his face.

While thinking of a response to this lunatic king, O'Reagan wondered how good it would feel to run him through with his sword. His hand began to move imperceptibly towards the hilt of his sword.

William was a skilled swordsman but he was no match for O'Reagan, the Irishman was a superb swordsman. O'Reagan's reputation as a warrior and skilled swordsman was known throughout the islands and as far as Scandinavia and Gaul. The list of men that drew a sword against him in anger and lived to tell about it was very small.

Sean was skilled enough in battle to know when to retreat and did so on this occasion, though it pained him greatly. "You may be right, William," he replied. "I will take your advice and bid you and your comrades a good night for I must prepare to leave for my land in the morning." Saying this he gathered his retainers and headed for the castle door. Turning back he said to William, "I have some advice for you, William, and that is keep that bloody assassin of yours on a leash, for if he's caught sneaking around my lands, I will return his head to you in a jar!" Turning again they stormed out of the castle.

During O'Reagan's outburst William had risen from his throne ready to challenge him. As he watched them leave, he bellowed for more wine. He said nothing as his silent court looked on.

Strathcon had been at the side of these proceedings watching the drama unfold and wasn't amused. He hated O'Reagan. William called him to his side and ordered him to take a dozen of his best archers and ambush O'Reagan, he wanted it done in Ireland, So that no blame would be attached to him. Changing his mind he then ordered Strathcon to stay and send his archers instead.

William wanted no blame to fall on Ian either as he still had uses for him. Obeying the king's wishes, Strathcon returned to court upset for he wanted to kill O'Reagan himself. He didn't like his remarks this night. As his hatred for O'Reagan ran deep over some mischances from the years before. His hatred ran deep for this man.

Staring at his court through drunken eyes, William would now have to keep his eye on Strathcon for he saw the contempt in his eyes when he returned. William wondered if there was anyone in his court that could truly be trusted. Slipping into a drunken stupor, he made for his chamber to sleep. This was William's usual condition for the headaches and paranoia that plagued him were only quelled by alcohol. His health began to deteriorate.

Farewells and Journeys

The evening before Liam and Wolf were to depart, the sultan ordered a farewell banquet for them. Jamie also attended.

It was a sumptuous feast; the sultan spared no expense on this feast. The entertainment provided was also first rate. Jugglers, dancers, fire-eaters, magicians, and acrobats kept the feast going into the early morning. They would sleep during the day and travel during the cool of night.

After their late night, the two young kings were ready to ride off and fulfil their destiny. A distraught Jamie was unable to join them as his wounds were far from healed. It would be a few months before he would be in any shape to fight or ride.

The usual joking around and farewells were over; a sad Jamie watched them ride off to the port, caravan in tow. He cursed his bandaged leg, and asked to be carried back to his quarters. He vowed to himself that he would meet his cousins at the appointed time and place or die trying.

His time healing would allow Liam and Wolf to complete their part of the mission and hopefully everything would fall into place when ready. He was not the best of patience and resented having to have people wait on him, something unusual to find in a future king. Rizhad and a few of his friends in the guard dropped by to visit and sometimes play chess with him.

The princess had left with her husband, so many nights he spent playing chess with the sultan. Chess was a game of strategy and the sultan was a master of the game. Rarely did Jamie win.

Several days later, while lying in bed, Jamie thought about all the adventures they shared in this land, when suddenly like a thunderbolt he understood everything. The sultan had played them, and played them well. From the first time they set foot in this land they were at the sultan's aid, with his cousins, they had saved the life of the princess, foiled a conspiracy to overthrow his rule, and helped unite a kingdom.

Well played, he told himself, the sultan managed to use outsiders to help make several slick moves within his kingdom. Should these moves fail, the blame would go on the foreigners, and traitors within his court would be revealed. After the beheadings, the sultan would rule as before. These were moves worthy of a chess master, they were brilliant. Well played!

Jamie was a fast learner and he would try and remember some of the things he had learned here for future use. Wounded, in both spirit and body, he had much to think about. Self-doubt now crept into his mind and he wasn't really sure they could pull this off. From a military standpoint, this was a huge undertaking as the distances involved were enormous and the risks great.

Healing now for a month, he still walked with a noticeable limp, but it was his mental state that concerned Master Po. While visiting one evening, he commented to Jamie, "You need to start training soon, if you don't you won't be in any shape to fight a prolonged battle. It will be difficult."

Everything is difficult, Jamie thought to himself.

Three days later, Jamie returned to the training hall and Po was happy. He knew in his heart that Jamie missed his family, and the princess, but for now his only concern was to make Jamie ready to do battle. Jamie trained lightly at first but once he regained some of his strength back, began working harder even though his wounds still bothered him a great deal.

During one training session, Jamie stumbled during a simple technique and a new student laughed at him out loud. Master Po was not impressed and without saying a word side stepped in front of the student and delivered a reverse roundhouse kick that sent him sprawling across the floor unconscious.

"Does anyone else feel like laughing?" he asked his now silent classroom. Nobody even blinked.

Kneeling over Jamie to see if he was all right, he observed the pain in his eyes, and blood coming from one of his wounds that had reopened.

"Training is over for you today," he commanded.

"No!" Jamie yelled, as he got to his feet. "I want to continue."

With mixed feelings, Po nodded, and ordered them to continue. Few men ever countermanded his orders and he gave Jamie a glaring look before his prize pupil passed out on the floor, and was soon carried away to his chambers to be attended to by the physicians.

Po was astonished at the tenacity of these men from the north and wondered if all the people from Jamie's homeland were like this.

One other quality that he admired was their courage. It's as though nothing but death can stop them, and even this they do not fear, it was astonishing to him.

Over the next few weeks Jamie's condition improved considerably and other than a slight but permanent limp he was nearly back to normal physically. Mentally it was a different matter. His heart was still heavy for he had no idea how the battle was going with Wolf and Liam. In fact he didn't even know if they were still alive. Languishing over the loss of the princess only compounded his problem. He must leave, and soon, he silently told himself.

The day before Jamie was to depart, the prince and princess returned to announce to the sultan that he would soon have an heir to his throne for Aza was pregnant. This news he didn't need to hear for the child was probably his. The sultan however was delighted and ordered a lavish feast prepared with the finest delicacies his chefs could produce.

The sultan genuinely liked the prince; he would be worthy successor for his throne. He had chosen wisely and Aza looked happy. He then introduced the prince to Jamie.

"So this is the young man that saved my wife's life, and helped unify our kingdoms, we owe you much. The last time I saw you, you were in fever and all the physicians believed you would be making a journey to the other world. I am so very glad that you were able to disappoint them," he said with a smile and a wink.

Prince Rashid then went on and told Jamie that along with his cousins Wolf and Liam, their adventures were being talked about around campfires from here to the borders of India.

"Your legend is spreading amongst the bordering nations as well. I am so very glad to meet you at last."

Grasping the prince's forearm and trying not to look embarrassed, he shook his arm and then told the prince, "I hope they don't exaggerate too much, Your Highness, as we may not be able to live up to their expectations."

The court laughed in approval and then the sultan spoke up. "All here tonight know the story of how these young men came to this court, and it is with great sadness that I tell you the last of these young princes will be leaving tomorrow, to return to his own land to reclaim his birthright. I have never had any dealings with these white-skinned traders from the north, but if they are all such men as these, I would welcome them as friends."

Turning to look at Jamie the sultan then said, "If for any reason your plans fail, my door is open and you are welcome here any time. I now want to give you this ring, show it to any of my border guards and you will be brought to me with haste and in safety. Taking his ring off, he handed it to Jamie, and then hugged him and returned to his throne. The wine had done its job and the sultan was getting visibly choked up and returned to his throne, he could say no more.

The prince now spoke up and said, "I have not been able to spend much time in the company of these men, but what little time I have spent with them I have enjoyed. Our conversations have been interesting and their skill as warriors is beyond question. I salute them and raise my glass in toast, join me." All in the court raised their glasses. "Saving the life of my wife is a debt I cannot really repay, so as a going away present I have brought several ships loaded with men and supplies, awaiting you in the harbour. As an extra bonus, I'm sending a contingent of Parthian bowmen with you," the prince announced. These were extraordinary archers that had an unusual way of fighting. This was a welcome gift.

Most of the men going on this adventure, unbeknown to the trio, had volunteered. Their legend was indeed growing!

Finally it was the princess's turn to speak. "These wild men from the north that saved the life of my maidservant and myself when all hope was lost, came to teach me some lessons of life that I will always remember. Perhaps some of these lessons will allow me to be a better wife to my husband and I wish to honour James with a token of my appreciation."

Leaning over she placed a large cut emerald hanging from a gold chain around his neck. Passing his ear she whispered softly, "I will love you always." Turning to the crowded court, smiling, she added, "Try not to lose your head in your coming adventures, or the emerald will have nowhere to hang." The court laughed.

While looking into each other's eyes for the last time, each was fighting off what they really felt, and it was the toughest fight either of them had ever experienced.

When the commotion died down and he was able to collect himself, Jamie spoke up and said, "My friends, I thank everyone for their kind words and generous gifts. I especially want to thank the sultan and Master Po for treating myself and my companions more like sons than guests."

A cheer rose up.

"If I am able to retake my throne and restore my family, it will be due to their efforts and teachings. I will take these thoughts and teachings into battle with me, and win or lose we will never forget the people of this land called Persia."

More cheers broke out.

"My companions and I will put what we learned here to good use. I thank you and farewell."

The crowd surrounded Jamie, and for the next hour he spent his time shaking hands and saying goodbye to nearly everyone in the court. Before finally going to retire the prince asked if he could speak to him privately for a few moments.

Jamie motioned for him to go to his chambers.

"James, I consider you a friend and I wish you well, but I must caution on one thing. The sultan has offered you a place here, but I would not accept his offer if I was you."

Jamie was a little confused by the remark and asked, "Why?"

The prince informed him that although they had made strong reputations, and made friends here, many in court resented their favour with the sultan. The prince's eyes said more.

Their eyes were locked in cold stares for a moment, and Jamie knew there was something more on the prince's mind. He then asked, "What's the real reason for this warning? I've played chess often enough with the sultan to know a feint when I see it."

Smiling, the prince answered him. "Let me put it simply, James. When two men are in love with the same woman, there is bound to be trouble."

"How long have you known?"

"From the first time I saw you in court, the way you two were gazing at each other said that you were much more than friends."

"I'm sorry," Jamie replied. "Just so you know the truth, neither of us planned this, but each of us knows our duty, and what we have to do. You have nothing to fear from me."

"Do not apologise, Jamie, she is a beautiful woman, and after what you went through together, it was no surprise. From the look on your face, I see that you still don't get my meaning. My wife is now pregnant, and it has come along very fast don't you think? If that child is born with red hair, it would mean that you would be put to death instantly, as would she. I am sure that you would not want this and if you stay this could change. Is my meaning now clear to you, James?"

After this explanation Jamie understood, and he was a little taken aback by it all. Could it be his child?

Jamie thanked him for his advice and understanding, and turned in for a fitful night's sleep. He was eager to leave this treacherous land and unite with his family.

Wolf and Liam had arrived in Denmark after an uneventful voyage that saw them carried to their destination by fair winds, and good weather. They had made good speed in getting there. They quickly made contacts and began arranging for ships and men to be recruited.

The small village they had landed at was one friendly to Wolf's father, they would be safe here. Wolf wanted to see his family as soon as possible. As soon as his magnificent white stallion that the sultan had given him as gift was unloaded, he made preparations to go there.

His father's village was only a few miles from where they now found themselves, and with Liam and a few escorts rode towards it after leaving instructions with his captains as nightfall was approaching. Nearing his father's village, he sensed something was amiss and told Liam to draw his sword.

The torches outside his former home cast shadows in the night and told Wolf that someone here was dying. He entered the lodge and bellowed to the servants: "My name is Wolf Larson and I want to know where my mother and father are."

One of the servants, Olga couldn't believe her eyes, for it seemed like only yesterday that she was changing his diaper and now this giant of a man stood before her. She said, "I am Olga, I don't know if you remember me, but he is on his deathbed."

Wolf recognised her and embraced her. "Take me to him at once!" he commanded.

Wolf entered his father's chamber and could scarcely believe his eyes. His once strong proud father had been ravaged by the disease, so badly he barely recognised him.

"What is wrong with him, and how long has he been sick?" Wolf asked, as tears began to roll down his cheeks.

"We do not know, master, it is some form of consumption that has been eating away at him."

"When did he become sick?"

"About a year ago, after he heard news that you might still be alive and living in a foreign land. The illness started slowly and then overcame him after several months; he has been bedridden these last three month. It is amazing that he was able to hang on this long."

Wolf knelt down beside his father and made a silent prayer to Odin, to allow him into Valhalla, the Christian equivalent of heaven. Why not, he thought? His father was a Viking before he was a Christian. Let Odin receive him. The Christian God left him in chains for three years, and for that he thanked no one.

While in prayer he wondered if his return would have any meaning now, or was it all for nothing? Still he was happy that his father knew he was alive. Suddenly the old man's eyes opened and seeing Wolf's face, he began to smile and then tried to speak but couldn't. The cancer that had wasted him away now robbed him of speech as well. He began to rise and then collapsed on the bed, and his life's journey ended.

Liam stood apart watching this tragic scene unfold and understood the pain his cousin was feeling. He could do little to comfort him, but tried anyway, with little success.

Wolf suddenly left the lodge and began questioning the servants and some members of the village that had gathered outside the lodge. He learned that his mother had died in the third or fourth year of his captivity, probably from the same thing that had just claimed his father's life. They could not be certain, and many said she died because she gave up all hope of ever seeing her only son again. She loved him so.

The servants were questioned a while longer and any that were slaves he set free. This caused an uproar among the village elders.

"How dare you!" they called out in unison.

"How dare you!" Wolf said, glaring at the group. "I bear the marks of lash and club across my back from three years as a galley slave. After that experience, I swore if I survived that ordeal, I would free every slave I came across. As of this moment, there are no slaves in this village, and any man that disputes this, can meet me in open combat whenever he likes."

Oddly no one came forward to dispute or challenge him as most in the crowd wanted to live to see the next day.

Wolf learned that although his father's small kingdom was not actually taken over, some key areas were controlled by men loyal only to William's gold. They would need to seize these ports and try and keep William from finding out at the same time.

That night, while talking to his father's captains and friends, Wolf learned that many of the Norse were beginning to grumble and many knew William's madness was becoming worse with each passing day. They were getting fat, lazy, and bored. William's gold was breeding contempt as well as jealousy.

Wolf's first question was, "How many men do you think we can raise in the next three months? Remember we need some time to train them in our tactics."

Eric, a friend of Wolf's father, spoke up, and said, "We can raise about two thousand in a month or two, leaving a good month for you to train them in your tactics."

Liam would need the time, as he would soon have to leave to arrange for their departure with the Gaulish sea captains.

Bjorn spoke up, and asked how many men Liam and Wolf had brought with them.

"One thousand," was Wolf's reply, adding that there were a few hundred volunteers in this village.

"That's ridiculous!" Bjorn shot back. "Do you honestly think twelve hundred men can fix the mess William created? Your uncle," he went on, "has at least three thousand men loyal to him here, and two or three thousand could be raised or bought very quickly."

The normally quiet Liam, now angered, spoke sharply. "The men that we have brought with us and the men we can raise along the way should be enough. The element of surprise and the tactics for battle we have learned in our absence will make the difference. The men we have brought with us are volunteers from the Sultan of Persia's personal bodyguard and all are seasoned warriors equal or better than any in this room. As we speak, trusted confederates of ours are making contact with new recruits and sea captains to arrange passage to Scotland for us. Jamie will be able to join us in a few months and we have to be ready. We must secure this kingdom before moving on to reclaim his kingdom."

Vladic, a man loyal to Wolf's father spoke up. "Why should we believe you, you speak of new tactics and battle plans, and ships, and yet you don't look like much of a warrior to me," he said, with a taunting smile on his face.

Wolf glowered at Vladic and began to rise from his seat after that last comment, when Liam told him to sit down.

Controlling his anger, Liam now taunted Vladic by saying, "I don't see why it matters to you, and after all, you're going to be paid a considerable amount of gold for your services. So why should you care?"

It was now Vladic's turn to get angry, and he asked Liam if he would care to try his sword arm. Liam's response wasn't quite what he expected.

"You're a big man with a big mouth, Vladic, so I'll try not to hurt you too badly," Liam answered.

They squared off and Vladic began to worry a little as when Liam removed his cloak and tunic he revealed a set of well-muscled arms nearly the size of his own. Considering Vladic was several inches taller than Liam this bothered him.

Angrily Vladic lunged at Liam, who quickly sidestepped the lunge, tripping Vladic sending him sprawling across the floor, sword clattering in his wake.

Liam now thought of what Master Po had told them of unbalancing your opponent, it works!

Those in the room watching this epic combat, and those that were now streaming into the lodge, were impressed and jostled each other to get a better view.

Vladic recovered quickly and again charged at Liam, who parried his blow and then reverse twisted his sword smashing the pommel into Vladic's nose causing it to bleed profusely. Bloodied and battered, for ten minutes he attacked Liam, but couldn't break down his defences.

Weakened he finally was in a position where Liam was able to deliver two snap kicks to the back of Vladic's knees, dropping him to the ground. Spinning around behind Vladic he smacked him across the back of the neck with the flat of his sword sending the big man to the floor unconscious.

Those watching the fight were very impressed as Vladic was a fierce warrior that few could boast about defeating in combat.

Twenty minutes later Vladic regained consciousness and after washing the blood from his beard and face, joined the others at the table. Giving his head a shake, he turned to Liam. "I hate to admit it, but you are the finest swordsman I have ever encountered, even if you are Irish," he said with a smile. "I'm sorry I doubted you, perhaps your plans will work, if the rest of the men under your command fight like you, I don't see how you can fail."

Liam then offered his hand and after a firm handshake, he looked him in the eyes and said, "If it's any comfort to you, Vladic," he said with a smile, "my arm feels like I was hammering at a rock and if the blood in it ever flows again, I might be able to continue this adventure."

The now crowded lodge broke out into laughter and Liam made a new friend that day, and one he could trust.

Once the laughter and commotion died down, Liam, Wolf, Vladic and a couple of other trusted men from the village, sat down and planned their moves. They would have to be careful, as Jamie had warned them, for William's spies were everywhere.

It was decided that Vladic would take about five hundred warriors with him and recruit along the way as they would no doubt have casualties as they fought battle after battle. He would attack the southern areas while Wolf and Liam attacked the northern ones, linking up when a larger battle was to be fought. The rest of the men they split up and scattered over and along the routes securing their supply lines and keeping the way clear for Jamie's arrival.

They would have to use the smaller well-sheltered coves along the way, for large fleets of ships entering Danish waters would be noticed and could cause some of the people in the area to raise the alarm, believing they were to be attacked. This was something they had to avoid for the plan to work.

Wolf's father was buried and after a short period of mourning, Wolf decided he would now live up to his name. Like a strong cunning wolf, he would strike his enemies when they least expected it, and most savagely.

Liam and Wolf hit each provincial town and coastal village during their campaign and quickly put to the sword any followers loyal to William's gold. Some villages and towns were easily taken and some put up a fierce resistance. Within two and a half months they had secured all the areas they needed. The way was now clear for part two of their plans.

To the south, Vladic had also been successful and soon the ports were secure and any ships that arrived from William's friends were seized and recruited as transport for their voyage.

This did not go unnoticed back in Scotland. William, although mad was not stupid, and noticed that his trade in weapons, slaves and contraband had slowed down and this caused him great concern.

Something was up, but what? None of William's spies had come to him with news and this was unusual. They were a greedy lot.

Unbeknown to William, one of the first things done was to round up William's spies. They were killed outright or locked away as it was imperative that the element of surprise be kept.

During their sweeps and battles, Wolf, Liam and Vladic made sure that these traitors paid the price for their treachery, but they would have to move soon, for sooner or later William would figure that something was wrong. The element of surprise was the key to finishing this campaign. They began to worry.

The Landing

The long journey was over and once again this desperate trio found themselves united in a just cause... Revenge! Liam had picked up a temporary, but slight limp and Wolf's left arm was bandaged up. They were banged up a bit, but still in fighting shape. After the usual hugging, and jostling around the three sat by the fire away from the rest of the camp drinking beer, eating, and discussing what they had accomplished so far.

Jamie was saddened to hear of the death of Wolf's parents because the three cousins had spent a few summers there and he remembered when they played in the cool clean air of the mountains and of swimming in the cold fiords. They would also generally get into as much trouble as they could along the way. How he longed for those carefree days again.

Liam informed him that over three thousand troops were pledged to their cause. Many that joined his ranks hated William, O'Reagan, and the assorted brigands in their employ. The rest that joined up just didn't feel like dying for a drunken, half-mad fool. Some of his recruits were loyal to Liam's father, and some had been friends. These men were trustworthy and were sent on ahead to secure food, horses, and men. They would also set up secure hidden bases in the forests and mountains.

It was decided when first planned that Wolf and Liam would hunt down and attack any gathering of William's followers that were on the way to join him.

This attack was decided upon to prevent any large concentration of William's troops from joining together to defend the castle or join up with William. They now saw the wisdom in their plans; by taking back Wolf's kingdom they now had a base to operate from. The ships they had captured, Liam would take on the voyage to his land when ready.

Liam and Wolf had changed the plan originally discussed for several reasons, and once explained to Jamie, he agreed most eagerly, they had done well. Their new plan made more sense as this way they could allow the Persian allies to stand down, for they wanted to finish the fight themselves. This was personal.

"Methinks you two have learned something from Master Po," Jamie said with a smile on his face.

"How so?" Liam queried.

"Well, I think it's a good plan, and if Master Po can train a couple of nitwits like you about tactics, then maybe this will work." Nearly laughing as he said it.

"Nitwits is it," Liam responded. "I think there is a man here known to some as a man of dung, which is fine among the heathens, but among civilized people we have a custom known as bathing." With that he looked over at Wolf, who was already grinning from ear to ear.

Wolf advanced towards Jamie with a speed that would astonish some and quickly had him in a bear hug and was walking towards the fiord.

"You cannot do this! I will be king soon, and you must act in a dignified manner towards me," he protested. Jamie put up a valiant struggle against the vice like grip of his cousin, but it was of no use. "I will have you beheaded if you do this!" Jamie shrieked.

Looking over at Liam, Wolf said, "I guess he's right, I should let him go, shouldn't I?"

"Unless you wish to walk around headless, I would do as he says, and obey your king," Liam replied.

"Very well I will let him go," Wolf said, and with that dropped him into the frigid waters of the fiord.

After several minutes of splashing and cursing, Jamie swam to shore only to find his friends and half the camp roaring with laughter. He soon found himself laughing along with them.

Once Jamie had dried off, the night fires were lit and after eating a hearty meal they sat around the fire discussing plans and events at the palace.

"Where is Rizhad?" Liam asked. "I thought he wanted to join our little party."

"His duties at the palace have delayed him but he should be arriving shortly," Jamie reassured them. "In the meantime we have much to do and get organised."

After an early night's sleep they set to work. Grain had to be purchased, ships loaded, and a million other small tasks had to be attended to. Liam and Wolf had wisely sent grain and horses ahead of their army. This would be stored by waiting troops that had been sent with the grain and horses.

The logistics of running an army were enormous and to try and organise it from several different countries and landing zones was a huge task. So as not to arouse suspicion, each boat was loaded and launched at different times. If William or any of his Norse allies had spies watching the ports, they wouldn't notice individual ships setting sail. A large flotilla of ships would be noticed and they would lose the element of surprise.

One week later Rizhad arrived with his contingent, and more supplies. "Hello my friends," he called out as they made their way into camp.

Once the usual horseplay and backslapping subsided they sat down and discussed events in Persia and of the coming battle.

Rizhad spoke up. "There were several in court that objected to this expedition and I fear that much of what the four of us accomplished at the palace in restoring order was for nothing. The traitors at the sultan's court constantly fight, argue, and plot, not that this is anything new. The princess is now with child," he added.

Rizhad looked over at Jamie and saw the colour drain from his face after receiving this news. He had expected that. Jamie excused himself from the circle and wandered off to think. They all knew why he left them, and they understood. While he was thinking Jamie wondered how she would react if the child was born with red hair.

Their lives were on different paths and each had a destiny to live, but that didn't stop it from hurting and Jamie couldn't help the way he felt. Life was unfair, he mused.

Jamie returned to the warmth of the fire and his friends. After a short time, Wolf decided that it was time to break the tension, which had descended over them.

"I don't know why, but it seems like whenever we meet a person that has travelled from the east for any extended period they always have a foul odour about them." All agreed and even Jamie began to smile again, for he knew what was coming next.

"I have to agree with you, Wolf, perhaps we should draw a bath for our new guests," Liam exclaimed.

Rizhad suddenly found himself staring into three sets of mischievous eyes and within moments found himself captive in Wolf's arms, and dragged to the edge of the fiord.

"If you infidels do this, I shall release a set of ancient curses that will shrivel your members for all time! Let me go or suffer the consequences, I warn you!"

Trying to keep a straight face, Wolf turned to Jamie and said, "You will be king soon and I await your orders, my liege."

"As your king, it is my wish to please my subjects. Since it is the wish of this fellow to be released, it is my command that you let him go," Jamie said trying to sound regal and serious.

Wolf dropped him and, after much screeching, cursing and splashing, Rizhad made his way back to shore. Wolf stood at the edge of the bank and held out his hand for Rizhad to grab and suddenly found himself flipped into the frigid waters.

After a generous amount of cursing, both were pulled from the water and returned to the warmth of the fire.

Food was brought to them and after the meal was finished they sat around staring into the fire.

Rizhad finally spoke up and said, "By the grace of Allah, that is the coldest water I have ever been in, my bones are chilled to the marrow."

"Well I guess you won't have to curse Wolf now for I'm sure that dunking shrank his member considerably, to be sure!"

They all roared with laughter at this. Each man staring into the fire wondered what the coming battles would bring. Who would fall? Would Jamie be able to retake his throne? What honours would befall them? Would Liam get his revenge? Maybe it was better not to think about it.

Rizhad left for a short time to see to the needs of his men and returned in a short while and rejoined the group. They were nearly ready, and in two days they would set sail to see what destiny had in store for them. They were all nervous, and anxious.

It was decided that Jamie and Rizhad would cross overland using an unused road in bad repair, and Liam and Wolf would land on the northern side of the island near the castle ready to attack if their original plan failed. It was Jamie's plan to call his uncle out to battle away from the castle.

This would not be an easy fight for William's troops were all battle tested, tough warriors. A roaming group of cavalry broken into groups of around twenty-five warriors would ride through the countryside causing as much confusion as possible.

The day finally came to sail home and they were all nervous and edgy. After what seemed like an eternity, they at last landed on Scottish soil. This was a feeling they would never forget or take for granted again. It even felt good to Wolf who had just come from his homeland.

The trick to this whole operation was in co-ordinating their attacks, using surprise to their best advantage, and keeping the enemy unbalanced. These lessons Master Po had drilled into them repeatedly. Jamie would use them to good effect.

Jamie knew how to unbalance William very quickly and that day while his troops were being unloaded, he began to work on a message sure to drive William crazy after reading it.

"What are you going to say to him James?" Rizhad asked.

"I've got something worked out, but I'm not sure it's enough to piss him off sufficiently. I'll read you what I have.

"Hello Uncle,

This is from you nephews James, Liam and Wolf.

You made a bad mistake in condemning us to slavery for we have survived and returned home to reclaim our birthrights, and to sever your head from your body.

You are a thief and a murderer, to think that a member of a royal household would turn on his own family, is beyond comprehension. However any that have sworn loyalty to you and lay down their arms will be free to go with no fear of getting an arrow in their backs, a favourite tactic of yours, I believe.

Should you gain a backbone and decide to meet me in battle, you can find me at the crows gathering."

"That's not too bad," Rizhad stated. "What do we do if he doesn't show up?"

"Don't worry, he won't be able to resist my invitation, his ego wouldn't allow it," Jamie assured him.

Being late summer the woods were filled with game and wild fruits in abundance. This was a good thing for Jamie's men could use some fresh food. It would also allow them to extend their own supplies in case something went wrong, or they were delayed for some reason.

The first day's arrival was a busy one as mass confusion and nervous captains unloaded their cargoes anywhere on the beach.

Rizhad was instrumental in sorting out the mess and soon some sort of order was instilled. Horses were fed and watered and sheltered for the night. Troops were fed and an anxious but tired army was soon fast asleep. They marched tomorrow.

The going was rough and slow for the first while as the road had fallen into disuse over the years and every hundred yards or so they would have to stop and clear away the debris and undergrowth. The local residents were very helpful as they were worried that William's conquests would soon bring him to their doorstep, any help they could provide would work in their favour.

Two hundred bowmen joined Jamie's forces and he was glad to have them for they were excellent bowmen and experienced woodsmen that knew this country. The condition of the road slowed them down for a while, but Jamie had allowed for this when he drew up their battle plans.

Although it was slow going, when they were done they would have a clear line of retreat to use if the battle didn't go their way. This was something Master Po had stressed, as he told them that all armies thought they were invincible until the moment when they were forced to retreat. Those that had an escape route planned lived to fight another day, those that didn't, perished.

There were many factors involved in winning a battle and the three young kings were paying their dues, and beginning to understand what they had been taught. Jamie was starting to have doubts about this whole undertaking, because it was incredible that they had made it this far without incident, even the weather had co-operated for them.

A few small fires were lit for cooking and warmth and while dreaming by the fire; Jamie's thoughts were of Aza and his unborn son. He worried that if the child was born with red hair, would she be stoned to death for committing adultery, and what would become of his son?

These weren't the thoughts that should be on a man's mind before going into battle, but he couldn't help thinking of them. He wondered if the other men in his army had similar thoughts about their lives and predicaments.

Rizhad joined Jamie at the fire and noticed that he wasn't quite himself, his mood, not being as it normally was.

"This country of yours is cold and wild, James, and I've never seen so many mosquitoes and bugs in my life," he stated. "How many more days before we dance with your uncle?" Rizhad asked with a wry smile on his face. His comments roused Jamie from his thoughts and he replied.

"Another day and a half march should bring us to where I want to fight this battle. My uncle has been informed of where he thinks I will be, thanks to the message I have sent him, and will no doubt try and get there ahead of us. His plan will not work for the place we have chosen to begin the conflict forces William to commit his troops to battle immediately with no preparation time, his forces will be in disarray."

Rizhad silently nodded his head in approval. "What's really bothering you, my friend? Is it the princess and your unborn son?" he asked.

Jamie was taken aback. "How did you know, Rizhad?"

"My friend, I am captain of the palace guard and there is very little that goes on there that escapes my eye, besides your friends and servants gossip a lot, I also have ears. The only thing I can't figure out, is how you managed to impregnate her? Since she is always watched, you must move like a thief in the night, in and out."

Seeing the expression on Rizhad's face made Jamie laugh.

Rizhad went on, "It does, however, explain why you never came with us when we were trolling for wenches in the market square."

"I'll bet you didn't know among the ladies of the night your cousin Wolf is known as the 'White Elephant'. I think it has something to do with the size of his trunk, or the colour of it," he said jokingly.

Jamie and Rizhad laughed for what seemed like hours and then Rizhad went off to sleep. Jamie stayed up for a while dreaming by the fire. They had been lucky so far, but Jamie was still filled with self-doubt. What he was feeling this night every other soldier, or general had felt at one time or another. He didn't like the feeling as this time he would be facing a family member. He was hoping to give William a few surprises.

After tomorrow's march there would be no fires, they would be running a cold camp from here on, so Jamie moved closer to the warmth of the fire. He longed to see whom if any of his family or friends were still alive. What would he say to them after an almost seven year absence? Could he show mercy to his uncle? These questions he had no answers for.

One thing for certain he knew was that a bad king was a bad king. He desperately hoped that he would be a good one.

The day before they entered William's territory, Jamie made camp and sent out runners and scouts to survey and gather any followers loyal to the true king. Liam had left word as to where to meet them. This wasn't too difficult of a task except for the fact that the clans were spread out over long distances.

William still had some loyal supporters and they saw about five hundred men riding towards William's castle. Jamie was impressed that this number of men would be loyal to a dog like his uncle. Now he wondered if these men were riding because the alarm had been given. Perhaps they had been spotted?

As William's men rode by, Rizhad commented, "This uncle of yours must pay out a lot of gold for the services of this many men, to come on short notice. He must be rich!"

"He supposedly has gold mines stolen from different families, mine included," Jamie told him. "He was always a miserable bastard and has probably gotten worse over the years."

While they were talking, a large group of mounted and foot soldiers joined them. These men had suffered under William's rule and were told of Jamie's return by men that Liam had sent to recruit forces. They were eager to join and fight. He was glad to have them, but wasn't expecting this number. Now he was concerned that their provisions wouldn't hold out.

Jamie received regular reports from one of his Scot-Irish scouts named Rory. Rory informed him that his sister was alive and being held at William's castle. Jamie was overjoyed at this for now he had some hope for his family. He was dismayed to hear that his uncle was planning to marry her in about a week's time.

Rory told him that the castle had been expanded and it would be difficult to take.

"I don't intend to take the castle," Jamie exclaimed. "In order to beat this army, we have to draw them into the open and make them think they are going to teach us a lesson. Don't worry they will come."

It was time to send his message to William; he only needed a messenger now.

Shortly after getting this news, there was a commotion amidst the camp and when Jamie and Rizhad came to investigate they were shocked.

Standing in front of them was Ian Strathcon, his uncle's favourite henchman. Now he had the perfect messenger. One of the guards told him they discovered him skulking around the camp perimeter and thought they should have a conversation. Jamie remembered his evil face, it hadn't changed much; in fact he looked more sinister than Jamie remembered.

"Let him go," Jamie ordered. "You shouldn't treat my uncle's friends in such a manner. He's our guest." In one swift gliding motion, Jamie moved and hit Strathcon with a right cross that bloodied his nose and nearly knocked him unconscious. When he got up off the ground, the mocking sneer on his face was missing.

Smiling at Rizhad all Jamie could say was, "Did that ever feel good. We don't like traitors in our camp, but I will spare your life. I may have a use for this piece of worm food, put him in chains and put a double guard on him," he said, smiling at the guard.

"You won't live very long whelp!" Strathcon yelled as he was being led away.

"Why don't you kill him now and save time, you know you're going to have to sooner or later," Rizhad told him.

"Maybe, maybe not," Jamie responded. "He can be used to deliver my message to William. After all, Master Po did tell us to improvise whenever possible," he said smiling.

Finally they reached their destination, the way was a little easier now and they soon made camp.

Jamie met with his commanders and drew up the battle lines that he wanted shortly after making camp. He was taking no chances with William, for he knew what a rotten scoundrel he was, and he was definitely full of surprises. Jamie allowed small fires to be lit for the night, as it would take William at least a couple of days to reach him.

Later that day, Jamie had Strathcon brought to his tent to stand before him.

"That murdering swine of an uncle of mine, the man you call friend, will be finished soon, and you can be thankful that your head hasn't been removed already."

"I have seen your puny army, and you won't live out the week. Your uncle has nearly four thousand men at arms, and

141

can call on another three thousand in reserve," Strathcon taunted him.

"Let me worry about my army, and any one of mine is worth ten of your soldiers," Jamie added sharply. "Right now, I need you to deliver a message to my uncle personally, no other is to read it. Understand?" Strathcon nodded, he understood.

He was blindfolded, given a horse and led out from camp a safe distance, untied, and sent in the direction of William's stronghold.

Jamie was taking no unnecessary chances.

William's only problem would be that he would be fighting a battle in a place he wasn't expecting. Jamie smiled to himself, as he knew how much this would piss William off. Strathcon would surely report on his 'puny' army.

While making the rounds of the camp with Rizhad later that night, he couldn't help being on edge. The culmination of six years of adventures that few men could imagine was nearly over.

Rizhad noticed Jamie's mood and tried to ease his mind. "Are you thinking of the coming battle, James?" He always called him James when he was trying to be serious.

"Of course," he responded. "It's not just that though, it's... everything, the princess, you, my cousins, the battle. I guess I'm just feeling apprehensive, it's been an enormous task to get here and I don't want anything to go wrong now."

"It's to be expected," Rizhad assured him. "Nobody can predict the outcome of a battle, all we can do is try. You should feel lucky my friend, for after this is over I have to return to that nest of traitors in my country. I don't even know if the sultan is still alive or if my country is at war. At least you're taking your country back. Your fate will be written in the stars."

"If it is, I'll need a translator to figure it out for me," Jamie said with a smile.

"You worry too much," Rizhad told him. "Besides most people would be scared to cross swords with someone that smelled like stable dung."

Laughing Jamie responded. "There's no way I can lose really, for after my enemies see your ugly face coming after them, most of them will probably die of fright."

After much laughter, two tired warriors went to bed with dreams of glory dancing through their heads.

Call To Arms

King William was in a rare good mood this night for he would soon be wed to a woman who had become more beautiful than her mother. The thoughts of Fiona's death still haunted him, how dare she disgrace him by her death. This one will never get the chance and will provide me with many heirs, he mused.

William's only problem at the moment consisted of his mines, which were becoming played out. He would have to find a new source of revenue soon or start spending his gold. This he didn't want to do. For the moment he didn't really care, life was good... or at least it was until his favourite henchman, Ian returned with Jamie's message.

Exploding into a rage, he called for his horse and armour to be brought and ordered a call to arms. Soon the trumpets were bellowing throughout the castle and people began to scurry around the castle like mad ants. William began pacing up and down, waiting for his armour, rage burning in his eyes like fire.

Staring at the floor, he then ordered his servant to send for the 'twins', and turning to Ian he said, "You were in his camp, what manner of army has this whelp?"

"His army consists of around two thousand men in total and he is understaffed in cavalry and bowmen from what I saw," Ian replied. "There is one thing you should know, and that is your nephew is not a whelp, he's grown into a fierce battle hardened warrior. Do not underestimate him."

What Ian didn't know was that Jamie had split his forces into smaller groups of men that would rendezvous at the chosen battle site. Ian was also unaware that Wolf and Liam were marching in their forces from different directions to link up with Jamie's forces. His army was expanding daily as new recruits were swelling the ranks daily. Most of those joining up were already battle hardened veterans, and when assembled would amount to over eight thousand men.

William stormed out of his chamber to hurry his troop on, if they were quick enough, they might get ahead of Jamie's army and gain the upper hand. Unfortunately he would be too late, for Jamie was already there, preparing some surprises for him.

Ian, although he was a coarse man, had over the years learned how to read and walked over to pick it up. After reading it he too tossed it to the ground and took off after William to stop him. Something in the tone of the message sent alarm bells off in his head… It looked too easy, something was amiss.

Jamie's message was quite simple and to the point. 'To the dog known as William Cameron, thief, and murderer, I, James Cameron, the rightful king of this land, have returned to reclaim my throne and inheritance. If you have the courage to meet me in battle two days hence, we can settle this, I'm looking for a new ornament to mount on my palace gate and have decided that your severed head would make a wonderful decoration'.

Jamie had learned much from Master Po… he had now unbalanced his opponent, and caught him by surprise. The battle was already in his favour.

The 'crows gathering' was a barren patch of ground in the middle of the kingdom with high cliffs on two sides marshes to the left and right, with rocky patches of ground strewn about. This was the perfect place to do battle for it already looked like hell.

William had sent runners and horse messengers out to his Norse allies while his troops were assembling, to enlist their support. Some of the Norse strongholds in William's kingdom were closer than he was and could arrive on the battlefield before him.

The response from the Norse wasn't exactly what William had expected. The Norse Jarls were divided as to how many men they should send for they didn't want to leave their territories and holdings vacant. The Norse scouts that had returned, reported seeing large bodies of wagons and men heading their way.

If the count was anywhere near accurate, this was a larger army than anyone expected and even if they combined with William's army it would be a hard fought battle. The question was soon answered for them, the alarm had been sounded, and they were under attack. Scrambling for their weapons and rushing out to do battle, they found they were under attack by around two thousand horse, foot soldiers, and archers.

Wolf had arrived. Wolf put in at a smaller cove to the south of the Viking settlement, unloaded his cavalry, and then loaded his archers, and foot soldiers onto the ships.

The sentries, unaware that a hostile force was aboard their own ships, were taken by complete surprise. Thinking it was men from their own village returning from a raid, no alarm was given.

This wasn't in the trio's original plan, but Po had taught them to adapt and when Wolf ran into an encampment of Norse warriors farther down the coast, he decided to slaughter them and use their boats to sail into the village. It was a gamble, but it paid off.

Wolf's troops attacked from all sides and in force causing confusion and panic in the Viking ranks. Most of William's friends were having trouble defending themselves and for the moment William's concerns were forgotten. They were now fighting for their own lives, and one of the 'jarls' sent a message to William that they were under attack and would he send what men he could, when he could.

The giant of a man leading the charge was a sight to behold. Smashing left and right from the back of a magnificent white stallion, anything in his path was cut down and the sight of it brought fear to even the most battle hardened veterans.

The battle did not go well from the very beginning for the Norse and two hours after it began it was over. Wolf's forces were superbly trained and disciplined; even so it was a hard fought victory.

When the fighting was over any of the Norse that hadn't been killed, were rounded up and put under guard. They would not attempt escape for their guards were Jamie's Persian allies, and they held no love for the Norse. They fought for glory.

Wolf ordered fires lit and food was cooked for the first time in several days. His men would rest and tend their wounds. Tomorrow they would begin the march to link up with Jamie's forces and should arrive there in another day. He secretly hoped that it would be he that killed William and not Jamie.

William received the message from his Norse allies and cursed them for their arrogance. Without his Norse allies, William couldn't hope to retain his throne. Suddenly he was very worried and broke off from the main body of his army and rode to the rear back towards the castle. Leaving orders with his captains before departing, he promised to return to the marching column as quickly as he could. William rode off in a fine temper. His captains knew him to be mad and never questioned his orders.

Rubbing a sore shoulder that had taken a terrific blow from the side of a Norse broadaxe, Wolf wondered how his cousins were doing and would everybody be able to link up in tine. They had been lucky so far, and he hoped that Liam was on his way back from the Irish coast with some fresh contingents of troops and or volunteers. The last few skirmishes that were fought cost some lives and equipment that needed to be replaced.

There was no need for concern as the stories already told about Liam and his cousins had spread throughout the islands, and Liam's ranks were swelling hourly. Groups of battle-hardened warriors had been arranged ahead of time to wait for Liam's arrival. They had been well paid for their services and wouldn't disappoint anyone. They were Irish … they liked to fight.

Liam had become a brilliant tactician and when making their plans, decided that their first attack would be on William's mine for two reasons; the first being much information could be gathered from the mine workers, and the second reason was even more important: this mine belonged to Liam's father, now it was his, now he was taking it back.

Landing at a small cove in Viking longboats about a half-mile from the mine, they marched in silence to the mine and then attacked in the early evening darkness. The defenders were taken by complete surprise and quickly overtaken. The Irish slaves forced to work in the mines were freed and fed.

Liam's forces gained another one hundred volunteers this day.

While sitting around the campfire that night, Liam and his captains noticed that several of William's friends had escaped. Things were going well, those that escaped would undoubtedly report to their lords and contingents of men would be sent out in the open, they would be easy prey for Liam's troops. He knew that they could not sustain a pitched battle against a fortified castle. Without siege engines and the enormous amount of supplies needed for a siege, it would be impossible to win.

Scouts trailed the escaped prisoners and reported to Liam, who had his troops lay in wait for any troops leaving the surrounding castles. They were cut to pieces by Liam's warriors.

To Liam, each of his warriors mattered to him, and he would never waste their lives on foolish adventures or risks. He had learned much from Master Po, and the sultan.

Leaving a small troop of his best men to guard what was now his mine, Liam ordered the men back to the ships and they set sail to link up with Jamie and Wolf. The winds were in their favour this night and they should make good speed.

He was worried for he was about a day behind and he was afraid he would miss the main battle.

Gazing at his Persian allies on the voyage across the channel, Liam was proud of them and wondered how it came that so many of them he considered friends. These were men from another land and yet they had become like family. He knew they would never betray him, they were proud fierce warriors and the stories they would tell of these adventures would be retold around their fires for many years to come.

William's supporters marched along, thinking they would have the upper hand and that it would be a short and easy battle. These were battle-hardened warriors that rode with William and during their many adventures and quests; scores of men had fallen under their swords and axes. Even his Norse allies were singing and boasting around the fires that night and challenges were thrown as to who would kill the most men in the coming battle.

In the morning William's troops marched around a bend in the road, planning to camp on the ridge and await his nephew, but were met with an astonishing sight. Jamie was waiting for them.

Jamie had on the previous night before the battle ordered his whole camp moved two miles east of the 'crows gathering'. This area had nearly the same defensive structure as the former with one or two exceptions, tall overgrown trees on both sides of the battlefield shielded Jamie's cavalry making it difficult to count their number. Archers were placed in strategic areas and spears were raised.

Informed by his own scouts and spies, Jamie ordered his troops lined up like cohorts of Roman legions. William now faced three long central columns with four smaller columns flanking these and a large body of warriors at the rear. Jamie had moved to this location to force William into battle, for now William didn't have time to set up his camp, he had to fight now or be wiped out. He had absorbed Master Po's teachings too. It paid off.

William rode closer to witness this for himself. Strathcon had been wrong. This was much more than two thousand men. Judging by the sunlight glistening off their armour and weapons, he estimated that they were outnumbered at least three to one.

The ranks of Jamie's original army had now swelled with new recruits and volunteers to almost six thousand men, all eager for a fight. Facing them William had about twenty-five hundred men and luckily they were battle-hardened troops.

William ordered his battle lines formed, keeping a safe distance back to avoid his nephew's archers. He was counting on his Norse allies for support and he wondered why at least some of them had not yet arrived. With this support, he could win the day.

William was unaware that Wolf and Liam's troops were marching towards him from different directions and that most of his allies had been killed or dispersed. All of William's spies and scouts had been killed or captured by Liam's men. He formed his lines, issued orders, and waited.

Before his lines were completed, the sound of trumpets and drums rang through the air. This was followed by a large group of black and purple robed men that marched to the front of Jamie's troops. The sound they made was an eerie one that cast a gloom over the battlefield on both sides.

On hearing the trumpets, Jaffar, and two of his companions that had survived the sinking with him, sat bolt upright in their saddles and rode with all haste to William. He was now facing a company of the sultan's 'Immortals'.

Jaffar spoke to him first. "My lord, we should leave the field of battle at once!"

"And why should I leave?" he enquired. "Are you frightened by the number of men we now face? I have fought battles outnumbering ten to one and have emerged victorious, fear not."

"You do not understand, my lord, those black robed men are members of the sultan's personal bodyguard, they are the hand-picked elite troops of his army. The men you now face have already killed many men in combat, they do not surrender; they give no quarter, and will fight to the last man. They also fight as a unit of ten thousand men."

"You must have better eyesight than I do, for I don't see any ten thousand men facing us. They are men and will bleed and die like any other men," William replied.

Jaffar was getting frustrated but continued on. "If the Sultan of Persia, whose flag I see flying in your enemy's camp, has sent these forces, it means he considers these men to be of the highest nobility and honour. The message is clear, if you win the day and slaughter his bodyguard, he will unleash the full might of his forces upon you and this your army could not withstand."

William stood up in his saddle, reached over and backhanded Jaffar across the mouth, nearly knocking him out of his saddle. "Do not tell me how to fight my battles or threaten me with tales of your sultan's military might or genius!" William screamed. "Now get back to your assigned position in the line and leave battle strategy to me. You are a snivelling coward and I should have told the men that rescued you from the sea to throw you back, you're too small to keep."

Sneering at William as he rode back to his men, Jaffar rubbed his sore jaw and then rode back to the rear of William's forces. They were assigned as part of a flying wing to plug any holes in the line. Signalling to his companions, they headed to the rear away from the battle. When some distance from the line they stopped to rest their horses.

While resting their horses and talking amongst themselves, it was decided that it was time to cut and run. This king was out of control and his armies would soon be in ruin.

Jaffar said, "That idiot king, who has kept us here against our will, has insulted me for the last time, we need to get a boat and see if we can escape." The other two agreed and they cautiously rode towards the castle at a slow pace so as not to raise any dust clouds that would alert William's men, who had no idea that William no longer controlled the castle or even that it had been attacked.

Riding along getting closer to the castle, the men sensed something strange in the air, and an uneasy feeling rode with them and weighed upon them heavily. Knowing they were in a cold harsh land that had suffered under William's rule, there would be nobody they could turn to for help. They were on their own.

Nearing the castle armed men suddenly burst from the brush surrounding them, bows drawn, and swords ready. To resist would have been useless, they would have been dead before they could draw their swords. They quickly surrendered their weapons and awaited their fate.

Liam had attacked the castle and found it lightly defended. It was almost too easy. His uncle might be a fierce warrior, but he was a lousy general. In William's haste he had probably taken every man he could round up to fight Jamie, never realising he would be attacked and overrun.

Once in charge of the castle, Liam made a quick tour of the additions and was astonished at the changes. For a moment he wished they were still kids and they could run and play all over these new areas of the castle. What trouble they could get into, he mused.

When entering the newly expanded king's chamber Liam caught a movement from behind one of the hanging tapestries in the corner of his eye and instinctively went into a roll, sword drawn as he came up, and found himself face to face with his uncle. His sword was also drawn. Momentarily stunned, he stepped back. Recovering quickly, he said, "Hello Uncle, Jamie will be most upset with me for he wanted to be the one that sent you to hell and now I fear I must do that honour for him. You are a murdering dog and you're going to pay for what you have done to this family!"

"That's brave talk coming from a galley slave," William replied. "You shouldn't have come back whelp, for it is you that will die here today." William grabbed a spear from a fallen soldier and hurled it at Liam, nearly pinning him to the wall

Ian Strathcon suddenly entered the chamber and now Liam faced two opponents. William's voice had sounded different to him after six years away from home. Perhaps his years of slavery had dulled his senses, he couldn't be sure. Removing his helmet and heavy armour, he then unsheathed his other sword and faced them both.

"I see you brought your camp dog with, you uncle, very well, I can slay two just as easily as one." He then attacked.

Liam's opponents were met with a flurry of two sword techniques, the like of which they had never seen before, and within minutes both his attackers were bleeding from several large gashes. He also knew that he could not keep up this kind of attack for very long, as eventually they would wear him down.

A moment later one of Rizhad's archers and a personal friend of Liam's, entered the room and put an arrow through Strathcon's heart and he was dead before he hit the floor.

Turning and smiling at Liam, Ardeshir called out, "This is now a fair fight, my lord," and then he left in search of other game, he knew Liam didn't need his help for most men that faced Liam's sword never lived long enough to tell about it.

"Surrender your armies now and submit allegiance to King James Cameron, and I will spare your life, if not, the buzzards will feast on your bones," Liam taunted his uncle.

This action only provoked William, which is what Liam wanted. An unbalanced enemy is easy prey. Master Po had taught them this, and they found it to be true.

To quote Sun Tzu, 'use anger to throw them into disarray'.

Boiling mad now, William charged at Liam, who quickly sidestepped and was shocked when William countered his move and nearly ran him through. Getting tired of this fight and anxious to meet up with Jamie and Wolf, he continued his two-sword assault with renewed vigour. Finding an opening, he lunged and dropped to one knee, driving the tip of his sword through William's throat. It was finally over... or was it?

Stepping back, watching the life drain out of the man, he had hated for six long years, Liam began to weep, not for himself, but for the lives lost, and for the cost of this foolish endeavour.

Although he didn't have a lot of time to spare, he made a quick inspection of the castle and was surprised to find a vast room filled with what he thought must be half of the wealth of the British Isles. Piled high were sacks of gold and silver coins, gilt bronze candleholders, jewels, furs, carved furniture, and a host of other objects of value.

This was no doubt the plunder and taxes William had coerced or stolen outright from his subjects. Then Liam opened another locked door, he was surprised to find Brigid, his cousin, and Jamie's sister. She was scared at first, until he told her not to be frightened and he was Liam O'Connor, cousin of the rightful King James Cameron. She began to cry and then looked at Liam with her arms outstretched and ran to him and embraced him.

Liam wasn't sure what to do at this moment and when she told him that she was his cousin Brigid, he embraced her and asked what had become of his mother. Sadly she told him she had come down with the coughing sickness two years ago and had passed on. This disturbed him, but at the same time, he was happy to see any member of his family alive. He knew Jamie would be thrilled.

After ordering some of the gold coin distributed amongst his men, he gave orders to march within the hour.

Leaving his wounded men to be taken care of at the castle, and a large enough force to guard it, they marched off at a quick pace in order to link up with Jamie and Wolf and finish this campaign. Two hours later, they met up and after the usual backslapping and greetings, they continued on.

Wolf was curious as to whom this beautiful, young woman was. When told she was his cousin Brigid, he couldn't believe it. The last time he had seen her, she was a scrawny little girl and before him stood a beautiful woman. He tormented her relentlessly as a child, but it was all in good fun. He rode over to her and embraced her, noting that she looked just like his aunt, Jamie's mother.

Liam had ordered Brigid to stay at the castle where she would be safe, but she refused and said she was going to see her brother and there was no way he was going to stop her. He had to relent and let her come with them. Liam told her that if fighting broke out, she was to ride to the rear of the column and ride back to the castle. He knew she probably wouldn't obey that order either, but he had to try.

Riding along she couldn't help but notice what a handsome man Liam had become. The lanky skinny little boy she remembered, had grown and become a large muscular warrior, whose legend was growing. She had heard tales from travellers of three young warrior princes, but had no idea it was them. For the first time in many years, Brigid felt safe and comfortable. Her emotions were all churned up, because for the first time in six years, she had family again. She had thought them all dead.

When Brigid thought of what might have been, had she been forced to marry her uncle and be forced to bear his children, she began to weep. Surprisingly it was Wolf that comforted her and told her that a new day was on the horizon and that her brother Jamie would reclaim his kingdom and sit on the throne.

Brigid couldn't believe the size of Wolf, he had always been a large boy who teased her relentlessly, but now he was a giant of a man. I wouldn't want to get into a fight with him, she now thought to herself, and I doubt if very many men would want to either. For the first time in many years, she found herself laughing aloud.

Liam was much different than she remembered him. He was very sullen and quiet, and this was not the Liam Brigid had known. What had changed him? She wasn't sure she really wanted to know.

Two hours before they were to meet up with Jamie, Liam's company was met by some advanced scouts bringing in prisoners, three to be exact. When the guards stopped to talk to Liam and Wolf, he thought he recognised one of the prisoners. Riding closer, he couldn't believe his eyes. The man he had wanted to kill for the last six years was now riding beside him. Could this be a trick of some sort?

Looking up, Jaffar now realised who this warrior was and the colour drained from his face, and he began to shake. Ordering the main body of his troops to march ahead Liam then ordered some of his troops to form a circle around him. Riding even closer to Jaffar, he rose up in his stirrups and kicked Jaffar off his horse, laughing as he did so.

Liam now took a sword from one of his men and slowly walked over to Jaffar. Pulling him to his feet, Liam cut the ropes binding his hands and then jammed the blade of the sword into the dirt. Wolf sat back watching this and wondered what Liam's next move was going to be. Would he toy with him like a cat that had just caught a mouse, or would he kill him quickly and move on?

Walking in a slow pace, Liam circled around him, confused as to what he should do to this wretch. He wanted to kill him, but he also wanted to make him suffer. For what seemed like hours, Liam paced around him, finally raising his voice to the heavens he shouted out, "I am now a firm believer in the Christ, for he has delivered unto me a dog I had thought drowned and long dead." At a quick pace he pulled the sword from the ground and threw it at Jaffar's feet.

A trembling hand reached slowly for the sword and after a short prayer to his god, he attacked with little success.

Jaffar's attacks were useless against a master swordsman like Liam and for the next ten minutes he toyed with this piece of trash. Finally an exhausted Jaffar crumpled to the ground. He was confused as to how a galley slave would learn to use a sword so well.

Breathing hard and covered in sweat, he screamed at Liam to kill him and be done with it. Raising his sword over his head to finish Jaffar and send him on his way to Allah, he hesitated and then turned looking at Wolf and said, "I can't do it."

For a few moments everything was silent as Liam stood over the body of the man he had wanted to kill for the last six years and, as he looked down at the prostrate form before him, he realised he couldn't do it.

"I'm not going to kill you for now, as I have thought of something better to do with you." Turning to one of his commanders he asked Darius if he thought his friend, the sultan could use some new oarsmen for his galleys.

"Why yes, my lord," he replied. "Just looking at him, I can tell that he is eager to become a member of the sultan's navy. Do not fear, we will see that he gets a window seat so that he may enjoy the scenic view."

Liam's companions broke out into laughter.

"Very well, tie him tightly, for he has a bad habit of escaping death. Let's be on our way as I'm anxious to meet up with Jamie."

After a few moments of riding along in silence beside Liam, Wolf finally asked, "Why didn't kill him, you've lived with that thought in your head for the last six years."

"I don't know," Liam responded. "When I held my sword over his miserable carcass everything we had endured flashed before my eyes and I couldn't do it. Perhaps Master Po was right; we must show mercy at times. I can tell you though, that I don't like it much," he said smiling at Wolf, and they rode on for a while in silence.

Wolf was astonished at the change in Liam, for he truly expected Liam to dispose of Jaffar in the cruellest manner, to show him mercy now was totally unexpected and baffling to him.

It had been a long journey home and one thing Wolf discovered along the way was that his cousins Jamie and Liam had become brilliant battle tacticians. They had planned this adventure and campaign by themselves with a few suggestions from Po. They were all eager for this to be over, as even warriors needed rest from battle. There would be other adventures in the future but for now, they just wanted to go home.

THE LAST DANCE

Jamie's archers opened fire with devastating effect and the first volley took out many warriors. Thinking they were out of range at about three hundred yards away, William's troops were surprised to see men and horses going down. They had no idea that they were facing Asiatic compound bows that could fire an arrow at over five hundred yards and beyond.

Amidst the sounds of dying men and screaming horses, William was perplexed; they were well out of range of bowshot. Was this something new? In minutes he knew that his battle lines would collapse and the day would be lost. He ordered his troops to pull back and hold the line while he returned to the rear to see what had become of his Norse allies. He headed for the castle.

After several volleys of arrows, Jamie marched out his troops from the left and right while his central columns moved forward at a slow steady pace. They were met by a fierce resistance from William's troops, which surprised Jamie. He then gave the signal for his cavalry to attack. Both flanks were hit and a flying column rode up through the middle of Jamie's ranks completely baffling the Norse who had never seen this kind of tactic employed before.

Faced with this new onslaught William's troops scattered and headed back towards the castle thinking they would be safe.

Following shortly behind William his troops ran across some bowmen from Jamie's forces and gave chase. For many of the men in this party it would be their last mistake. The men they were chasing were 'Parthian bowmen'. These men were skilled horsemen and this runaway tactic had been used for many years with great success. Such was the skill of these men that while at a full gallop they could turn and fire arrows with deadly accuracy.

The few men that were left horsed turned and rode off in an easterly direction far away from William's castle and this battle. This was a decision that saved their lives for they had never seen tactics like this used before in battle and they were unnerved by it all.

Jamie released the rest of his forces and William's troops were soon defeated. It was over! His troops were now busy rounding up stragglers and disarming any survivors. He gave the signal for the victory trumpet to be heard.

Sitting on the back of his horse he heard the cry of the ravens over the battlefield. Screaming a Keltic battle cry across the valley that unnerved some of his own troops he knew the day was his and the journey over. Surely the ravens were a sign from heaven!

During the battle Jamie couldn't lead the cavalry charge with Rizhad being pressed with command decisions. Rizhad went on without him and now Jamie was worried that something had happened to him.

During the first minutes of battle, Rizhad charged William's lines swinging his sword in large arcs and was cutting a large swath in William's lines before an arrow caught him in the shoulder knocking him off his horse. He went into a roll as Po had taught them and came up sword at the ready. Breaking off the arrow embedded in his shoulder he signalled to his commanders that he was all right and for them to continue on.

By the time Jamie had caught up to Rizhad he had liberated another horse from a Norseman and rode to Jamie and informed him of his uncle's departure, seeing that Rizhad was wounded he asked him to stay back and look after things on the battlefield.

Nodding and smiling at Rizhad he gathered eight men to ride with him and they all changed over to fresh mounts. Rizhad knew this was a fight he couldn't attend anyway, as this was a personal matter between Jamie and his uncle.

Jamie and his men rode off at a full gallop as he went to settle a score with the man who had caused so much misery to many people's lives. The quest would soon be over and there was no way he was going to let William get away with this.

With their fresh mounts they quickly overtook the few guards that rode with William and although they put up a valiant fight soon surrendered. Jamie was riding alongside William and then leapt from his horse and the two fell to the ground in a great cloud of dust. Taking off his heavy armour and helmet as he rose from the dust, he could now move more freely.

William arose slowly and the two began to circle each other like predators looking for an opening from which to attack.

Taunting Jamie, William said, "So the galley slave has returned home to die, so be it." He then lunged at Jamie who managed to sidestep the blow. His uncle was a good swordsman, he remembered, and he would give William no mercy. This was a fight to the death.

"Once again, uncle, you are wrong, for it is you who will die here today, and well you should pay with your life for the misery and dishonour you have brought to this family. I've dreamt of killing you for six years and now my quest is almost over and this time you're going to pay!"

Boasting that he had over three thousand Norse allies on the way, William thought this would impress Jamie... It didn't.

"My scouts reported to me that your Norse allies were destroyed, and, your castle or should I say my castle is now under my control. You have no allies left and most of your army is destroyed, and I intend to put an end to this nonsense today. Make your peace."

Suddenly William's face turned blood red and even the colour of his eyes seemed to change. He lunged at Jamie with the fury of a mad bull, cursing at the same time.

Jamie noticed something strange about his uncle as he dodged his blows but he couldn't figure out what it was.

William was a strong swordsman and pressed his attack on Jamie with everything he had.

After ten minutes of thrust, parry, and dodge Jamie was feeling the pressure of his attack and was starting to get fatigued. This wouldn't be an easy victory.

William made a large two-handed swing at Jamie thinking he would catch him off guard. Jamie had been waiting for this and dropped to one knee driving the point of his sword deep into William's chest. A shocked William clutched his chest and then fell to the ground, dead.

An hour later Wolf and Liam rode in not noticing the body which lay a few feet from where Jamie was sitting. Jamie was half lying, half sitting on the ground trying to collect himself. He was exhausted and the adrenalin rush that had kept him pumped and going all day was beginning to wear off.

Dismounting their horses three, tired, bloody men greeted and hugged. Wolf informed Jamie that he was now king of his castle and that his uncle was dead. Before a startled Jamie could respond a beautiful red haired woman rode up to him.

"Who's this?" he asked.

"It's your sister Brigid," Liam replied.

She dismounted her horse and walked slowly towards Jamie and then broke into a short run and embraced him like a lost lover.

No one was more surprised than Jamie, tears rolled down both their cheeks and it was some time before either of them could even speak.

Then the tears and hugs and words were over, Jamie looked at Liam and asked, "What did you say before Brigid rode up? Did you say uncle was dead? How did you know that I killed him?"

Wolf and Liam looked at each other in dumb surprise at this remark.

"I know uncle is dead because I killed him myself back at the castle some hours ago."

Now it was Jamie's turn to be surprised. "It can't be!" Jamie protested. "For I killed him not more than a couple of hours ago and his body lies right over here."

Quickly the three ran over to the prostrate form of William lying on the ground and tore off his armour. Cutting open his tunic they stood back confused as to what they were seeing.

William had a large unmistakable scar running down his right shoulder, and this corpse had none. What was going on?

When William was first given instruction in the use of the sword an overzealous instructor slipped during a training session and sliced open William's shoulder.

Jamie then mounted his horse and suggested they ride back to the castle with a small bodyguard and investigate this further, something wasn't right. Not knowing that his father's castle had been renovated, Jamie was astonished to see the change.

Liam led them to the chamber where he had dispatched William and kneeling down rolled the corpse over and it was indeed William. Tearing off the corpse's tunic and exposing the shoulder there was no scar to be found.

Three very confused young men stood in stunned silence as they tried to figure out this new development.

"What in the hell is going on?" Jamie asked. "If both of these imposters aren't William, then who are they? And where is William? Has this all been for nothing?" He then said, "When I sent this one to the otherworld there was something strange about him and I couldn't figure out what it was at the time, but now I remember. The one I killed, his voice wasn't the same as I remembered, and it was high pitched. I remember uncle with a deep scratchy voice."

Jamie ordered all the castle servants that were still alive brought to him for questioning, there had to be an answer to this.

"Do any of you know the real identity of this man? Speak up, no harm will come to you as I am your rightful king and ruler and this castle now belongs to me."

One elderly servant named Rory MacLellan spoke up and said, "They are twin brothers, my lord, your uncle discovered them on one of his raids and they were brought back and raised as his twins, and used on several occasions."

"Who trained them in the use of the sword?" Jamie asked.

"He did, my lord, reasoning that in order to pull off the deception they would have to learn how to mimic his gestures and mannerisms, including how he used the sword."

"You mean that dog lives!" Wolf blurted out. "Where could he have run? We have all the roads and trails covered."

"He could have escaped by sea," Jamie said. "Send scouts to all the nearby ports. If they find anything report to me at once."

Jamie ordered food prepared, the wounded were brought into the castle. Fires were lit and for the first time in six years he would sleep in his own castle tonight. Rizhad was brought in his wounds were bandaged and tended to, all the while him cursing that he was taken out of the fight too soon.

"So James you are now the king of your castle, how does it feel, my friend?" Rizhad asked.

"To tell you the truth Rizhad, it's sort of a hollow empty feeling right now, that and the fact that I'm tired as hell," Jamie responded. "I've got my sister back and that's a start, I don't know what it will take to restore my kingdom or how long it will take to sort out William's misdeeds. It does feel good to be home at last."

"You will make a fine king," Rizhad said, "As long as a filthy dung warrior like you stays downwind of your subjects you will be fine." They all laughed.

With a smile on his face Jamie looked at Rizhad and said, "Just another five inches to the left and I wouldn't have to listen to you anymore, it just shows how poor Scottish archers have become in my absence if they can't hit a slag like you,"

After the laughter subsided it was a tired army that went to sleep early this night. Jamie hoped his riders would bring him news of William's whereabouts for this wouldn't be finished until William had been put to the sword. For now all they could do was wait and see where he would turn up.

The next day Jamie inspected his castle and was astonished at how much it had been expanded and enlarged. The improvements pleased him. His main concern now was to round up the remnants of his family. Restoring the injustices plaguing his kingdom would take time.

Never far from James Cameron's mind were his thoughts of the princess and his son. Oh... how he longed for her, knowing in his heart that time would heal his wound but it would be long and painful journey and he wondered if he would ever find a love like that again. He wasn't sure if he wanted to go through anything like that again, that kind of pain cut deeper than a sword.

They had travelled far and seen many things, and like all men noble or common they learned the hard truths that life offered up.

Rizhad said I would be a good king, he mused to himself. Time would answer that question for him. One thing was for certain, the Cameron clan would be known throughout the land as fierce swordsmen, and brave warriors for many centuries to come.

EPILOGUE

Two weeks after the final battle, Rizhad and the rest of the wounded Persians were sufficiently recovered to travel and would be leaving soon. Many of the Norse and Persian allies had returned home already.

The feasting and celebration that went on the night before their departure would be talked about around campfires for many years to come.

While riding to the docks Jamie, Liam, and Wolf rode with both joy and sadness in their hearts. They would be saying goodbye to Rizhad and their Persian friends along with the adventures they had shared for the last three years. They were home and home they would stay, it was over.

Dismounting their horses these four rough, tough warriors from four different cultures embraced and tried to hide the fact that they were welling up with tears.

Walking slowly to the gangplank Rizhad turned to his friends and said, "You three are the best friends I have ever had and I will miss you all very much. Castle life won't be the same without you. For me it has been an honour to fight at your side and share in your adventures. I hope the god you pray to keeps you well and safe. I will ask Allah for a special blessing for you."

Turning to Jamie, Rizhad said. "As for you, James Cameron, you are the best friend I have ever had and I now fear for you as I will not be here to protect you anymore."

They all laughed.

"Alas I must return to that nest of serpents in my country. Goodbye my friends, I hope I never have to face any of you or any of your countrymen in battle for you are fierce warriors and men of honour."

As the three cousins watched Rizhad walk onto the ship the last three years of escapades flashed before their eyes.

Sadly a few centuries later these nations would face off against each other when the bloody crusades began.

***

During the attack on William's castle, no one noticed the small ship that pulled out of the harbour jetty, destination Norway. The cloaked man rubbed his right shoulder; the old battle scar was throbbing and bothering him this night. Perhaps the dampness, he thought to himself.

Many hours later when the small ship reached port, William's madness began overtaking his rational thought. He began to curse Jamie for returning, and his mother for driving him mad. Still thinking he was king; he tried to act the role.

After tying up and disembarking he called over to some large muscular men he assumed were dock workers as they were unloading cargo from a boat.

"You there," he called, "come over here and unload my cargo at once, both of you now!"

The two men looked at each other and shook their heads. Quizzically, the large black men responded by asking, "And who might you be that we should unload your cargo?"

"I am King William of Scotland," he replied with a crazed glassy look in his eyes.

Both men couldn't believe what they were hearing, the large white man then spoke up and said, "Since you are the King of Scotland we will gladly unload your cargo and see to it that it arrives safely at your new destination. There are many thieves, robbers, and other perils of the road that my partner and I could protect you from for a small fee."

Stepping closer to fish some coins out of his pouch he grumbled to himself how one always had to pay these beggars when it should be reward enough serving their king.

Vladic stepped closer to receive the coins from William and then drew back and hit William with a hard right across the jaw that knocked him cold.

William woke up in the hold of an old open skiff where his boat and cargo should have been. He was furious and began to rant and rave. "How dare they!"

Three days later, William tracked them down in a small tavern about thirty miles from the harbour. Screaming furiously at them he demanded his cargo. After many curses and blood oaths, Vladic finally drew his sword. Quickly the tavern cleared out. This fight was clearly in Vladic's favour and William began to lose ground quickly. The constant throb in William's sword arm from overuse was causing him excruciating pain.

Vladic was by far the superior swordsman. The two slashed, cut and parried for a good ten minutes before William made his last mistake. William made a lunge thrust that Vladic easily sidestepped driving his sword through William's ribs.

While William lay dying, Vladic leaned over the once king, and said, "My friend James Cameron will be happy to get back your cargo and see that it gets back to the people you stole it from. However I fear he will be very angry with me for he wanted to kill you himself! May you rot in hell!"

As the last breath of life left William, he cursed them all. The madness had won.

A few days later Vladic and Eskandar would return William's treasure and Jamie would in turn return it to the people.

James Cameron would go on to found a dynasty that became known for their fierce swordsmanship. He would rule his small kingdom fairly and his people would see to it that the legend of his conquests and battles continued on. Except for the memory of his lost love, his reign was a happy one, with many more adventures along the way.

Wolf would return to his lands, already a legendary warrior, he too would have many more adventures and conquests.

Liam would restore the trouble in his small kingdom, and go on to become one of the finest warriors to ever come out of Ireland, eventually killed in battle when he was very old.

Rizhad returned home to continue in the Sultan's service; he was eventually killed during a palace coup many years later.

The love of Jamie's life, Aza and her son were killed during the palace coup that nearly took Rizhad's life. All over a throne that Jamie never coveted, it was such a waste. The usurpers wanted no red haired claimant to the throne. Jamie never knew.

This group of intertwined lives would learn the lessons of life and love that all men must learn, and they would learn that all men must fulfil their destiny whether it is for good or evil. This is not to say that one cannot change their destiny, or can they?